A King Production presents…

All I See Is The Money…

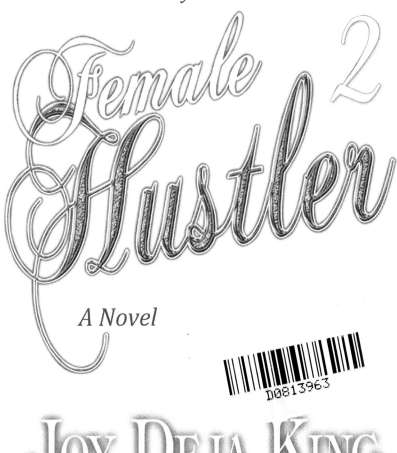

Female Hustler 2

A Novel

D0813963

JOY DEJA KING

ISBN 10: 1942217102
ISBN 13: 978-1942217107
Cover concept by Joy Deja King
Editor: Jacqueline Ruiz: tinx518@aol.com

Library of Congress Cataloging-in-Publication Data;
A King Production
Female Hustler Part 2: by Joy Deja King
For complete Library of Congress Copyright info visit;
www.joydejaking.com
Twitter @joydejaking

A King Production
P.O. Box 912, Collierville, TN 38027

This Book is Dedicated To My:

Family, Readers and Supporters.
I LOVE you guys so much. Please believe that!!

—Joy Deja King

"Hurt me with the truth. Don't comfort me with a lie..."

~Rihanna~

A KING PRODUCTION

All I See Is The Money...

Female 2 Hustler

A Novel

JOY DEJA KING

Chapter One

Like Father Like Daughter

"Get us the fuck outta here!" Nico barked to one of his men as he held onto Angel tightly. The barrage of bullets continued to fly through the empty warehouse, but none seemed to be aimed directly in their direction, which made it easy for Nico, Angel, and his men to make an escape.

"I'm over here!" Angel yelled out when she recognized one of Darien's bodyguards blasting his weapon in the distance. "Let me go!" she screamed at Nico, trying to squirm out of his grasp, but his grip was too strong.

"Do you want me to shut her up, boss?" one of Nico's men questioned ready to put a bullet in Angel.

"If you touch her, you're dead," Nico warned.

The stern coldness of Nico's voice sent a shiver down Angel's spine. She looked up at him and wondered for a brief moment why he was being protective of her. She quickly dismissed it as Nico simply needing her for collateral.

"Boss, you all head towards the back exit now. Carlos is in the truck waiting. Nathan and Tony will stay with you. Me and the rest of the men will handle things here," Elijah said to Nico. "When I nod my head, you all go and I'll cover you."

A few seconds later, Elijah nodded his head setting off an endless round of shots as Nico, Angel, and the two men darted towards the exit. From the corner of her eye Angel saw the bodyguard she recognized heading in her direction. Right when she was about to attempt to kick Nico and make a run in the bodyguard's direction, she saw a bullet blast through his neck. He put his hand up to cover the hole, but the blood gushed through his fingers and the next shot sent him to his knees. Angel put her head down knowing there was no way Darien's bodyguard survived the onslaught.

When they finally made it to the awaiting SUV, no words were spoken; Carlos the driver simply sped off once everybody was inside.

"Do you want us to tie her back up?" Tony asked Nico once they were in route.

"No, let her be. She won't try anything, will you, Angel?" Nico turned and said to the young woman he believed to be his daughter.

"No, I won't try anything." Angel folded her arms and scooted over so she could put space between herself and everybody else. She stared out the window trying to escape into her own world if only for a short period of time.

"What's up with Nico? He sure is handling that girl with kid gloves," Tony commented to Nathan in a low tone.

"I just do what the boss says and don't question him." Nathan shrugged as they both eyed Nico who was on his cell, engrossed in a phone call.

They seemed to be driving forever. Angel was trying to stay awake so she could see where they were going, but the smooth ride and the stress of the days events took their toll and she soon found her eyelids getting heavier and heavier. Before long she had fallen into a deep sleep.

"What happened... where am I?" Angel muttered when she opened her eyes. She'd almost forgotten that she had been kidnapped and nearly killed in a barrage of bullets less than twenty-four hours ago. But when she saw the tall man with a dominating presence sitting in a chair across from the bed she was sleeping in, the memories came flooding back.

"What are you doing in here with me! You didn't rape me did you?" Angel mumbled with fear in her voice and eyes. She grabbed the blanket and pulled it up to her neck.

"Of course not," Nico stood up from the chair and said. "I would never hurt you. I put you to bed myself."

"My clothes are intact," Angel smacked, looking down seeing she was still wearing the same clothes from yesterday. "So I guess you're telling the truth."

"I am telling the truth. I have no interest in harming you, Angel, and I won't let anyone else harm you either."

"Why are you being so nice to me all of a sudden? You wasn't talkin' all this I won't hurt you shit yesterday when you had your men yank me off the street like I was some trash."

"I apologize for that."

"Well, if you're so sorry then let me go home."

"I can't do that yet."

"I knew you were full of bullshit. Trying to act like you so concerned about my well-being. You're using me to get to Darien aren't you?"

Nico remained silent not responding to Angel's question. He walked with purpose back and forth across the multi-colored Agra marble floor. It gave the open-spaced bedroom an exotic yet contemporary look, but also very comforting.

"You don't have to answer me, but I already know the answer. I recognized one of Darien's bodyguards before your men shot and killed him. The only reason he would've been there was if Darien sent his men to get me away from you."

"It's not that simple, Angel," Nico said shaking his head slowly back and forth. "Why are you with a man like Darien Blaze anyway?"

"Excuse me! Is the man that had me kidnapped and almost killed really questioning my taste in men? Get the fuck outta here," Angel barked rising up from the bed. She was now standing; ready to walk up on Nico as if she could beat him. "First you bring up my mother, now you're asking me about my man. What do you want from me? Whatever it is spit it out so we can get this bullshit over with."

"You really shouldn't talk like that." Nico frowned.

"Talk like what?" Angel questioned with confusion on her face.

"Using words like fuck and bullshit. You're a beautiful young lady there's no need to speak like that."

"Are you serious right now?" Angel folded her arms staring at Nico in disbelief. "Dude, I'm a grown woman and last I checked my mother and grandmother were both dead and you ain't my daddy so why in the FUCK," she yelled, making sure to emphasize the word fuck, "are you trying to tell me how to speak. It's bad enough you're holding me hostage so please spare me the parenting tips."

"Listen, I understand we're not meeting under the best of circumstances, but while you're here I want to make you're as comfortable as possible. I'll have Margaret bring you some clean clothes and you can tell her what you want to eat."

"Who is Margaret?"

"She runs this house for me... takes care of everything. Whatever you need, she'll make sure you get it."

"Well can she get me a ride up out of this joint?"

"I guess I need to clarify. Almost whatever you need," Nico chuckled. "Please feel free to take a shower. Everything is in the bathroom. Watch television; listen to some music just try to relax. I'll be back later on to check on you."

After Nico left he stood in front of the closed door before locking it. Although in his gut he believed Angel was his daughter, he didn't want to get ahead of himself. Yes, she had an uncanny resemblance to his ex, Lisa, and there was also the birthmark they both shared, but it could all be a crazy coincidence he tried to rationalize. If Angel was his daughter, then he would have to make some adjustments regarding how to handle the Darien situation. If she wasn't, then Nico would proceed with his original plan which more than likely meant Angel was a dead woman.

"Mr. Carter, is everything okay?" Margaret asked when Nico came into the main house.

"Yes, everything is fine. I have someone staying in the guesthouse. I want you to bring her some clean clothes, comb, brush, get her whatever she wants to eat. When she's done, bring her stuff to me."

"Will do, Mr. Carter," Margaret smiled before walking off to take care of her boss's request.

After his conversation with Margaret, Nico wasted no time heading to his office to get back to business.

"Boss, I was looking for you," Elijah said coming out of Nico's office.

"Good because I was looking for you too. Follow me." Once the men entered Nico's office the first thing Nico did was pour himself a stiff drink.

"What's the next move regarding Darien? Are you ready to put the call in letting him know if he wants his girl back then he needs to pay what he owes plus interest?" Elijah asked.

"No, don't place the call."

"Oh, you wanna skip that step and jump right into sending him one of her fingers or a ear or something and have it delivered to his front door in an envelope? I mean he knows we have her so no need prolong this shit." Elijah shrugged.

"No, don't do that either."

"So what, do you want me to put an ambush in motion? I got your men lined up, they're just waiting to get word from me," Elijah said confidently.

"I want you to hold off for a second."

"Hold off on what?"

"On everything," Nico said pouring himself another drink.

"But why?"

"Because I said so."

"I'm not trying to question your decision, boss," Elijah said not wanting to upset Nico. "You were just so adamant about shutting Darien down and now you're saying to wait."

"I'm waiting to get some important information before I decide how to proceed."

"How much time are you talking about? We don't want to get caught off guard and Darien try to make another move on us like he did last night."

"True, so make sure you double or triple up on security. Also, try to find his location so we can have a set of eyes on him at all times. Hopefully, it won't take long to get the information I need, but I'll keep you posted."

"Then I'll wait for your orders," Elijah said about to leave.

"One more thing," Nico swallowed hard before setting down his glass.

"What is it?"

"Besides Margaret, I'll be the only one dealing with Angel unless I tell you otherwise. Keep the two guards outside of the guesthouse, but they have no reason to go inside to see her unless I say otherwise. Also, make sure the men are being watched on the security monitors at all times. Not so much as a strand of hair better be out of place on her. Are we clear?"

"Yes, boss. It's handled," Elijah reassured him.

Once Nico was alone, he held up a picture of his daughter Aaliyah and sadness spread across his face. She was still missing and he had no clue where she could be. And now there was a chance that he had another daughter and Aaliyah had a little sister.

"We have to get you home baby girl. Wherever you are, I will find you," Nico vowed.

Chapter Two

The Waiting Game

"Damn! I almost had her. We were so fuckin' close!" Darien balled up his fist and yelled before pounding down on the granite counter. He kept circling around the island in the center of the kitchen spewing every curse word he could think of.

"Blaze, you need to calm down," his driver Keaton advised.

"Don't tell me what the fuck I need to do. My girl being held by that motherfucker Nico and I was this close to getting her back," he huffed showing a small space between his thumb and index finger.

"We'll get Angel back and next time we'll be better prepared. We didn't realize he would have so many men with him. We're lucky we only lost one," Keaton reasoned.

"I swear on my life if anything happens to Angel I won't stop until I kill Nico myself."

"It won't come to that," Keaton said out loud, although he wasn't sure he didn't want Blaze to know that.

"We don't know shit. That nigga hasn't even reached out to tell me what the fuck he wants so I can get my girl back. The number I had for him don't even work no fuckin' more. He playing the waiting game. I haven't even slept since Angel went missing," Darien admitted, choking up. "This shit is all my fuckin' fault."

Darien Blaze was a championship boxer built of solid muscle, but at this moment he appeared beaten and weak. The pain and guilt of losing Angel seemed to have drained him of all his strength.

"Man, you have to pull it together. I've known you most of my life. We grew up together. You have to stay focused. We gon' get Angel back. We do what we do. Always have and always will."

"This is different. Nico a different type of nigga. Fuck! I should've listened when he told me he either wanted his money back or his drugs," Darien said shaking his head. "I tried to play that nigga like he was a clown and look what the fuck happened. Who looking like the clown now."

"Yo, don't blame yourself man. He gave you some bad drugs. You did the right thing not paying that man."

"Get the fuck outta here! We both know that Chucky and them niggas be bullshittin'. Chucky probably just told me that shit knowing I would take his word for it 'cause he my cousin. But that shit don't matter. I should've just paid him. Ain't like I didn't have the money."

"Stop being so hard on yourself. This ain't yo' fault." Keaton was trying to make his friend feel better, but it wasn't working.

"Never did I think he would come for Angel. He went straight for my heart and ripped that shit out." Darien leaned down on the kitchen counter and put his head down as if he had already begun the mourning process.

"The clothes seem to fit you well." Margaret smiled as she watched Angel standing in front of the living room window wearing a Boho chic halter with flirty lace and a breezy open back. The mint blue color of the dress blended with the ocean sea Angel was staring into.

"Yes, they do, thank you," Angel replied not taking her eyes off the ocean front view.

"The view is beautiful isn't it? Very soothing. It's as if looking out into the water takes all your stress away. I brought your dinner."

"You can just leave it on the table."

"I know you said you didn't want any dessert, but I brought you some anyway. In case you change your mind."

"Thanks."

"If you..."

"Look," Angel said cutting Margaret off before turning around to face her. "I'm sure you're a nice lady and you've been nothing but kind to me, but I'm not interested in engaging in a conversation with you so you can go."

"You're talking to me and not through me so I would say that's progress." Margaret gave Angel a warm smile. "Mr. Carter told me to watch over you and I plan on doing exactly what he asked."

"Do you do everything Mr. Carter tells you to do," Angel mocked.

"I try to make sure all his expectations are met. He is an excellent boss and I take pride in meeting his demands. He's also a very good man."

"Oh really? Do good men have women dragged off the streets and held against their will? No matter how fancy the accommodations," Angel said sarcastically as she looked around the three-bedroom, three-bath private guesthouse that had a Floridian villa resort style feel. "Oh Miss Chatty Kathy did I hit a nerve. You're quiet as a church mouse now. Can't think of what to say to defend your boss who is such a good man."

After staying silent for a few more minutes, Margaret finally spoke up. "I don't get involved with Mr. Carter's personal or professional dealings. I run his home and do what I am asked. But I will say that Mr. Carter must have a very good reason for having you here. He also must think very highly of you."

"Why would you say that?"

"Because he told me to go out of my way to

make sure you're comfortable and have whatever you need. Also, no one else besides him is allowed to see you but me. For whatever reason he seems very protective of you," Margaret revealed.

"Thank you for dinner and dessert, Margaret. If I need anything else I'll ring for you," Angel said ready for the older woman to leave. In a strange way Margaret reminded Angel a lot of her deceased grandmother. That was one of the reasons she gave her the cold shoulder. Under the circumstances she didn't want to soften up to the woman. Margaret had a sweet deposition that made you welcome her presence. Angel wasn't sure if Nico was using the woman as bait to get her to open up so she was being cautious.

"My pleasure, Angel. Please don't hesitate to reach out to me if you need anything. This might not be your ideal living arrangement, but I'm here for you," Margaret said sincerely.

Angel believed that Margaret genuinely meant what she said, but she still didn't trust her. As far as she was concerned Margaret worked for the enemy and that was Nico Carter.

Angel sat down at the table in the dining room to eat her dinner after Margaret left. She thought about what the woman said. Mainly that Nico thought highly of her and seemed protective of her. Angel couldn't help but wonder why.

This man doesn't even know me. He never laid eyes on me a day in his life until we came face to face at the warehouse. Why would he be so invested in my well-being? Then he mentioned my mother like he knew her. Could he have known my mother? Times like this is when I would give anything to have my grandmother here with me. She would break this shit down to me like a detailed science project. Or maybe whatever his beef is with Darien he wants to make sure I'm not harmed because he doesn't want things to escalate even worse. Hell! I don't know. None of this makes sense. The only person who can give me the answers I need is the man himself. Yep, I need to switch shit up and get Nico Carter to put his guard down and open up to me. That's exactly what I'm going to do, Angel thought to herself as she took a bite of her seared citrus glazed salmon.

Chapter Three

Moment Of Clarity

Taren was growing impatient waiting to hear from her inside source. The last she heard, her supposed best friend Angel had been snatched up off the streets of Miami. She had plotted meticulously to make it happen and all seemed to go as plan. Now all she wanted to know was if Angel was dead or alive. She had agreed not to call her source and just wait for him to reach out to her, but the suspense was driving her insane. Taren was even tempted to make a house call to Blaze, but didn't want to run the risk of getting interrogated by him and fucking up her story. She had spoken to him briefly on the first day Angel went missing, but hadn't heard a peep out of him since.

"Taren! Girl don't you hear me talking to you?" Aspen shouted, snapping her fingers in Taren's face.

"Sorry. I have a lot on my mind."

"I bet you do. None of us have heard from Angel in days. The rest of the girls are starting to get worried. Nobody was been working and it's not like Angel to not handle her business. I hope nothing bad happened to her." Aspen sighed.

"Yeah, she should've reached out to us by now. I am getting worried."

"It's crazy because you were just saying that Angel wouldn't be around much longer to run the business and now she's missing."

"Aspen, I was just running off at the mouth. I didn't mean anything by it!" Taren snapped. The last thing she needed was Aspen repeating that to other people and suspicion falling on her. "I would never want anything bad to happen to Angel. She's my best friend."

"I know that that, Taren," Aspen said reaching over the restaurant table and patting Taren's hand. "I was saying what a crazy coincidence that was. I guess that's why they say be careful what you say because you can speak things into existence." Aspen shrugged before pouring some more ketchup on her already drenched French fries.

"I didn't speak anything into existence. One thing has nothing to do with the other," Taren barked defensively.

"Calm down, Taren. Nobody is blaming you for Angel's disappearance. For all we know maybe she got into an argument with Blaze and needed to get away for a few days. Maybe that's why he called you because he thought she was staying with you or you knew where she was. It's not like he would want to tell you they had a falling out."

"That's very true, Aspen. I wouldn't be surprised if that's exactly what happened," Taren agreed happy that Aspen was coming up with alternative scenarios on her own. She didn't care who was blamed for Angel's disappearance as long as it wasn't her.

"You don't think that Blaze would physically hurt Angel do you?" Aspen leaned in and whispered. "What if him calling you and being concerned about Angel was all just a ruse to cover his tracks because he hurt her?"

Aspen was now in full conspiracy mode pointing all fingers towards Blaze and Taren was ecstatic. She fed right into Aspen's outlandish theory because boyfriends killing their girlfriends was much more common and plausible then what had really transpired on the day Angel went missing.

"Aspen, I really think you might be on to something."

"You think?" Aspen's eyes widened as the idea of Blaze hurting or even killing Angel was becoming more real to her.

"Yes. I mean it makes a lot of sense. That idea never even crossed my mind until you brought it up and you might be right."

"What should we do? Maybe we should go to the police and tell them what we think. If Blaze hurt Angel then his ass needs to be locked up!"

"Let's wait a minute," Taren put her hands up not wanting a hyped up Aspen going to the police with her suspicions, especially since they were dead wrong. Taren worried that if the right detective started investigating he could easily find out that she was the one actually involved in Angel's disappearance and not Blaze.

"Why should we wait?" Aspen wanted to know.

"Because we can't just go around making accusations like that without proof. We'll give it a couple more days and see if Angel contacts us. Like you said maybe they did have an argument and she went out of town for a few days to clear her head. If we haven't heard anything in a few days then we'll go to the cops. Okay?"

"Fine," Aspen reluctantly agreed.

Taren was keeping her fingers crossed that within the next couple days she would hear from her inside source. Now that she let Aspen unleash her Blaze murder conspiracy theory, she would not be able to contain her. Taren didn't need the trouble since she was up to her neck in the mess. She had to find a way to keep Aspen in line before all the lies blew up in her face.

"Thank you for seeing me," Nico said when he sat down on the living room couch across from Angel.

"This is your house did I really have a

choice?" Angel huffed, rolling her eyes.

"Of course you did. I had Margaret ask if you would be willing to see me and you could've said no, but you didn't and I appreciate that."

"I don't want your appreciation I want answers. I want to know what's your beef with Darien and more importantly why are you being so nice to me? None of it makes sense."

"I'm not in the position to discuss that with you yet, but I will say no matter what happens, you need to get Blaze out of your life. He is the reason you're here."

"At least you finally admitted that. What did Darien do that was so bad that you would resort to kidnapping?"

Angel could tell by the expression on Nico's face that he was battling whether to answer her question or dodge it. For the first time Angel felt like she was making inroads with Nico and didn't want to lose the momentum.

"I think I deserve to know why my life has been turned upside down. Although I believe what you've done to me is unforgivable, you seem like a decent man," Angel said hoping her soft-spoken approach would strike a sympathetic cord with Nico.

"I had some business dealings with your

boyfriend and he screwed me over."

"Screwed you over how?"

"Money." Nico was getting pissed just thinking about how Darien tried to play him.

"Money? How much could it be? Darien is rich. I'm sure he has more than enough money to pay whatever he owes. I thought you were going to tell me the truth. Don't feed me a bunch of lies."

"Angel, I am telling you the truth. You're still young, but the longer you live and the more you experience, the more you'll understand how men like Blaze operate. It's not about the money it's about him constantly needing to stroke his own over-inflated ego."

"You don't know anything about Darien. He loves me and he would never do anything to put my life in jeopardy."

"But he has. He's the reason you're here. When he wouldn't pay what he owed me I had to take something he valued away from him which was you. So he has put your life in jeopardy, Angel."

Angel couldn't sit down any longer. She walked over to the huge bay window and stared out at the water that had now become her source of solace. She didn't trust Nico, but her gut instincts were screaming he was telling the truth about Darien.

"Darien is a boxer. What sort of business dealings could the two of you have been involved in? Are you some type of boxing promoter?" Angel wanted to know more. She was tired of trying to put the pieces to the puzzle together and needed more answers.

"No I'm not a boxing promoter, but I prefer not to get into all of that."

"Why? Unless the business dealing was illegal." The way Nico's body shifted in the couch, Angel felt she was on to something. "Wow, you're a drug dealer," Angel stated without hesitation. "You must be very high on the totem pole to be living like this."

"Angel, you're treading into territory you know absolutely nothing about."

"I actually know a lot more about that territory then you think. Gavin, the man I considered to be a mentor and even a father figure in a lot of ways, was in the same profession. He wasn't on your level. Clearly you're on some kingpin status, but Gavin did very well for himself. He taught me all about the drug game. If it wasn't for him, I would've never learned how to be a good hustler. So trust me, I know plenty."

"You said that this man named Gavin was

like a father figure to you. If you don't mind me asking, what happened to your biological father?" Nico inquired.

Angel rested her head against the glass window knowing that the subject of her father was a touchy one. "I never knew my father."

"Really, why is that?"

"Because my mother died giving birth to me and the identity of my father died with her. I have no idea if he's dead or alive." Tears began to swell up in Angel's eyes. No matter how hard she fought it, she was unable to stop them from trickling down her cheeks.

"I didn't mean to upset you, Angel. I apologize." Nico wanted to walk over and comfort her, but held back.

"No need to apologize. It's not your fault I don't know who my father is, therefore never had a relationship with him."

"Still, you're upset and I hate my prying into your personal life caused it."

"When you first saw me that night at the warehouse you asked me was my mother's name Lisa. How did you know that?" she questioned while wiping away her tears.

"You reminded me of a woman I used to know named Lisa."

"Was it my mother?"

"I'm not sure."

"Oh," Angel couldn't hide her disappointment. "It may sound crazy, but I was kinda hoping you did know my mother."

"Why is that?"

"So you could tell me about her. Before she died, my grandmother raised me and she showed me tons of pictures of my mom. She always shared cute little stories about my mom and how we looked so much alike. But it would be cool to hear stuff from someone who knew my mother in a different way," Angel shared.

"It must've been hard on you growing up without a mother or father," Nico commented in a concerned tone.

"It was," Angel acknowledged nodding her head. "Growing up I was so jealous of my best friend Taren because she was so close to her father. He spoiled her rotten and I always wished I had a father that would do the same for me. It wasn't until Gavin came into my life that the void was somewhat filled. But no one can take the place of your real father," Angel divulged.

"I lost my own father at a young age. Unlike you, I did have a chance to know him, but the day he was shot and killed still haunts me. You've experienced a lot of loss at such a young age and I can relate to that."

"You're right, I have experienced a lot of loss, but when I least expected it my life was filled with lots of love, too. Darien changed me for the better. For so long I was scared of love and honestly wasn't sure if I was even lovable, but Darien showed me otherwise."

Before Nico could respond, Margaret interrupted them. "Mr. Carter, an important package just arrived for you. I placed it on the desk in your office."

"Thank you, Margaret. I'll be over to the main house shortly."

"No problem, sir."

Nico turned his attention back to Angel once Margaret left. "I enjoyed our conversation. You opened up to me. I feel like I got to know you much better."

"As if you care about getting to know me. I'm just your hostage no need to pretend it goes any deeper than that."

"It might go much deeper than that, but we can have that conversation another time. If you don't mind, after I handle a few things I would like to come back so we can continue our discussion."

"I'm game, Mr. Nico Carter."

"Then I'll see you again shortly." Nico smiled.

"What just happened?" Angel asked herself out loud once she was alone.

Angel would never admit it to Nico, but she enjoyed their conversation too. She was very tight-lipped when it came to her personal life, but Angel connected with Nico and was able to express her most private thoughts with ease.

"What the hell is wrong with me! I can't possibly be developing a friendship with the man who is holding me hostage. Is this that Stockholm syndrome I read about? Gotta be." Angel laughed before flopping down on the King-sized bed. For the first time since this ordeal began, Angel was able to laugh and she was actually looking forward to Nico coming back for a visit.

Chapter Four

The Chase

"Damn, nigga! I've been waiting for you to call me. What took you so long?" Taren snapped when she answered her phone.

"Calm down. Shit been crazy over here. This the first chance I had to call you. Nico has us on lockdown."

"So what's up? Is Angel dead?" Taren jumped right in, not wasting any time.

"Nah, she's still alive."

"What! Why? I thought the plan was for me to deliver you Angel so you could then kidnap her and that Nico would then have her killed because of his drama with Blaze."

"I thought so too, but Nico changed shit up on us."

"I'm confused, Tony. I delivered on my part, you delivered on yours so you telling me Nico is the holdup?"

"Yep! That's what I'm telling you. Listen, this shit got me confused too. That man did a one eighty and can't nobody figure out why."

"So where is Angel now?"

"Staying in the guesthouse on Nico's estate. I haven't even seen her since we brought her here. Nico won't let nobody near her."

"Oh really." Taren paused for a moment and tapped her nails on the bedroom nightstand pondering what Tony said.

"Hello!" he barked after there was silence on the other end of the phone.

"I'm here. I'm trying to figure out what changed for Nico."

"I don't have time to sit on this phone wit' you while you do all that, but if you figure it out, let me know," Tony said looking around the room he snuck into to make sure nobody was listening to his phone call.

"Hold up, Tony!" Taren yelled in the phone not wanting to let him hang up since she had no idea when he would call back.

"What is it?" he huffed sounding agitated.

"We have to get Angel away from Nico since he's the reason she ain't dead yet."

"Is you crazy! I ain't doing all that," Tony barked.

"What you mean? Shit, maybe I need to call that Nico cat myself and find out what the hell is going on," Taren mumbled under her breath. Tony didn't know it, but one night when he had fallen asleep at the hotel she went through his phone. Taren knew the code because being a nosey bitch is one of the things she did best. Something told her to write down Nico Carter's number because she never knew when a powerful man like that could be useful to her.

"The only reason I went along with your plan was because I thought it would score me some cool points with my boss. I ain't 'bout to lose my life for you. For whatever reason, if Nico want that girl alive, then that's what it's gon' be. Now I have to go... bye!"

Taren's mouth dropped when she looked at

her phone and realized the call had ended. "I can't believe that motherfucker hung up on me," she screamed into her cell. "Unfuckin' believable!"

Taren didn't know what had her more pissed, the fact that Angel was still alive or that Tony had punked out on her. She shook her head in disgust at how her master plan seemed to be blowing up in her face. Taren thought she had hit the jackpot when she came across Tony. He had been a client. Although he wasn't rich like most of Angel's customers, he was willing to pay. After the third time he hired Taren for her services, she asked him did he want to save a little money by cutting Angel out the mix and dealing directly with her. Tony was game and started hitting her up two or three times a week.

Soon their sex hookups turned into long hours of pillow talk. On one of those occasions Tony slipped up and started discussing his boss, Nico Carter, and how Blaze had fucked him over and Nico was going to bring him down.

When Taren informed Tony that Angel was not only Blaze's girlfriend, but also her best friend his eyes lit up like a Christmas tree. That's when they began orchestrating Angel's kidnapping. Nico had been trying to figure out a way to break Blaze down and when Tony informed him he could deliver his girlfriend, Tony felt like he was now the man. Taren figured with Angel out the way she could take over her business. Tony promised he would bring her some rich clients, all she had to do was make sure she supplied nothing but bad bitches.

Taren began counting the money before she even made any. She felt she was in a win-win position: get retribution for her father's death—which deep down she always blamed Angel for—and get rich running a high-end escort service. Now her dreams of having it all seemed to be slipping right through her fingers.

"Fuck that!" Taren yelled at the bathroom mirror while staring at her reflection. "I've come too far to let Angel come out on top. Since Tony couldn't get the job done, then it's up to me to finish it and get rid of Angel once and for all."

When Nico picked up the envelope from his desk, an awkward fear shot through him.

He wasn't use to this uncertainty and being scared of the outcome almost kept him from ripping open the packet.

"Fuck that!" he barked anxious to see what was inside. When Nico had Margaret bring him Angel's belongings he handed over what was needed to run a DNA test. The results were now in from the lab and Nico would get the truth. As Nico opened the letter, he realized how crushed he would be if it turned out he was wrong and Angel wasn't his daughter. "I knew it!" he shouted, when the results revealed he was in fact Angel's father.

"Nico, can I speak to you?" the knocking on his office door and the sound of Elijah's voice brought Nico's celebrating to a halt.

"Sure, come in." Nico was tempted to share the good news of finding a daughter he never knew he had with Elijah, but opted against it. He wanted Angel to be the first to know and Nico was eager to tell her.

"Boss, we have a problem."

"What sort of problem?" Nico questioned coming from behind his desk.

"We lost connection with the guards assigned to watch Angel."

"What do you mean lost connection?"

"We can't get in touch with them."

"Did you look a the security monitors?"

"That's the thing. I had Tony outside the door

guarding it, but he stepped away for a second. When he got back the door was wide open, the monitor was off and Nelson was gone."

"What the fuck happened to Nelson?"

"Not sure, but I have some of our men looking for him right now. The moment Tony told me what happened I came to tell you."

"Has anyone gone to check the guesthouse?" Nico wanted to know.

"Yes, I already sent three of our men to investigate," Elijah informed him.

"Come on! I need to know what the hell is going on over there." Nico grabbed the piece of paper with the paternity results on it and rushed over to the guesthouse.

When Nico and Elijah reached the guesthouse they were greeted with two dead bodies lying in a pool of blood. Without saying a word, Nico charged towards the front door that was wide open. His heart was racing and the only thing that kept running through his mind was that only minutes ago he learned he had another daughter and instead of him being able to rejoice the news, she had been ripped out of his life.

When he stepped inside the guesthouse, Nico's fears were confirmed although it was better than what he initially thought. Nico expected to walk through the door and find Angel lying in a pool of her own blood like the men that were supposed to protect her. Instead, Angel had vanished. There was no trace of her.

"She's gone, boss," Ellis, another one of Nico's men revealed. As more workers came in they all remained silent, sensing that Nico might explode at any moment. None of them wanted to feel his wrath.

"What the fuck happened! Two of my men are dead, Angel is gone, and Nelson has vanished. I want some fuckin' answers now!" The bass in Nico's voice seemed to have the room vibrating.

"Boss, everything seemed straight until Tony told us that Nelson was gone. Never did we think we would come here and find dead bodies or the girl you was holding hostage gone. I don't know what else to say," Nathan said before putting down his head.

"I guess none of you knuckleheads have anything to add. And where the fuck is Tony?" Nico barked as his eyes darted around the room.

"I'm right here, boss," Tony said, raising his hand like he was in elementary school.

"You better have a damn good reason as to why you abandoned your post." Nico was seething and everyone in the room wanted to take cover.

"I only stepped away for a second to use the restroom," Tony lied. "When I left my post all was good, but when I came back...." Tony's voice trailed off knowing he was lying through his teeth. He had snuck off to call Taren and that's when shit went to shambles.

"We should've killed her when we had the chance," Ellis said casually. "Ain't no telling who has her now."

Without hesitation, Nico reached over and snatched the 9mm out of Nathan's hand and pounded the gun into the side of Ellis's face, crushing his jaw and knocking out a couple of his teeth. Blood gushed from his mouth and he bent over on the floor in excruciating pain.

"Don't you ever say no shit like that again or you a dead man," Nico spit, leaning over Ellis with the gun pointed in his face. "If I hear some shit like that from any of you... you're all dead men," Nico warned as he made direct contact with each man standing in the room. "Elijah, I want you to use every resource we have to find Angel and for all ya's sake she better be alive."

"I'm on it right now, Sir."

"Now get out of my face. Each and every one of you... you make me sick!" The men scrambled to get out of the guesthouse as quickly as possible, almost leaving Ellis behind. Tony and another worker came over and had to basically carry Ellis out as his blood continued to drip leaving an exit trail.

Nico stood in the center of the room incensed and emotionally devastated at the same time. Both of his daughters were missing and he had no clue of what to do.

Chapter Five

Forgive Me

"We got her, Boss. We're headed to you."

When Darien received that call from one of his henchman, it felt like his blood had begun flowing again, as if he was no longer dead and had been brought back to life. He didn't want to ask until he had Angel back in his arms, but he prayed she hadn't been hurt in any way. It seemed like an eternity since she had been away from him and after her traumatic experience, he knew Angel would never be the same again. As he waited for her arrival, Darien's cell began ringing. He figured it was his people calling back so he didn't even bother to see who it was before answering.

"I know it was you that had your men come into my home, take Angel, and kill two of my men in the process. I'm willing to give you a pass for killing my men, but I want Angel back here ASAP," Nico demanded.

"Even in defeat you still a bossy motherfucker. I ain't giving you shit. I should have yo' ass killed for kidnapping my girl, but I'll spare your life just stay the fuck outta mine."

"And here I thought you would've learned your lesson by what happened, but I guess you don't know what I'm capable of. Underestimating me will be your downfall."

"Nigga, fuck you! Nah, you the one that's underestimating or have you already forgotten my men came up in yo' spot?" Darien chuckled. "But I tell you what. We both busy men and there ain't no sense of letting a lil' miscommunication make shit escalate even further. So I tell you what, I'm willing to pay the money you claim I owe you and we can call it even. What you say?"

"You can keep the money just bring Angel to me. If you do that, then we're even," Nico countered.

"Is you fuckin' crazy or is this a joke? Either way you can remove Angel from the equation 'cause it ain't gon' happen."

"You're making a huge mistake, Blaze. I'm coming for you."

"Catch me if you can, motherfucker!" Right when Blaze ended the call he heard his front door open. He rushed towards the foyer and there stood Angel. They seemed to run towards each other in slow motion.

"Baby, you're home," Blaze said squeezing Angel tightly. "I'm never letting you get away from me again."

"Don't worry, I'm not going anywhere."

Blaze lifted Angel's face up and when their lips touched, his heart melted. This was the moment he had been waiting for and honestly thought it would never happen again. Blaze was thrilled that he was wrong.

"I take it Blaze turned down your offer," Elijah stated when Nico got off the phone.

"You damn right. His pompous ass ain't learned shit."

"Nico, let me ask you something."

"Go 'head." Nico was reading over the paternity results again so he was only partly paying attention, but that didn't stop Elijah from talking.

"Why the sudden change?" Nico was so engrossed in what he was reading that he didn't hear the question until Elijah brought up Angel's name. "Why the sudden change when it comes to Angel? One minute you were willing to use her as bait to get your money from Blaze and now you're turning down the money in exchange for getting Angel back. It makes no sense. Normally you're always about money and business. What has changed?"

"These aren't normal circumstances."

"Then tell me what's going on so I can understand."

"Some things aren't meant for you to understand and this is one of them," Nico explained.

"I've been part of your organization for years. I consider myself to be your most loyal worker so what possible reason do you have not to confide in me?"

"Elijah, you have been extremely loyal and I also trust you as much as I'm capable of trusting another individual. But I'll never confide everything to you or any other man."

"I see. I'll let you get back to what you were doing and I'll continue working on getting Angel back."

"That's a good idea." Nico could tell when Elijah got up to leave that he was angry, but Nico wasn't ready to let anyone know about Angel yet because he felt it would put her life in danger. With the life he lived, Nico knew he was always a target and that included his loved ones. Angel was now his family and he had to protect her at all cost.

"Angel, will you ever forgive me for what I put you through?"

"Darien, will you stop asking me that. I don't blame you for what happened to me, but I would like to know why you were involved with a drug dealer."

"How do you know Nico is a drug dealer?"

"Although he didn't come out and tell me I was able to figure it out. He said you owe him money. Why didn't you pay him?"

"Because I'm stupid. There really isn't a better explanation than that."

"Well, I need one."

"I have a cousin and some old neighborhood friends that sell drugs. I supply them by getting the drugs from Nico."

"But why? You don't need the money."

"The money isn't for me, it's for them."

"Oh, it's your way of staying cool and being down with your so-called friends in the streets."

"I guess you can say that," Darien replied feeling somewhat embarrassed by the admission.

"Don't let your so-called friends bring you down because trust me, they won't be around when shit hits the fan. You still haven't told me why you didn't pay Nico," Angel continued.

"My people said the drugs were bad so when Nico asked for his money I told him I wasn't going to pay for some bad drugs. So he told me to give him back the drugs, of course I didn't have it." Angel wasn't saying a word, but her facial expression was speaking for her. "I know... I know... it was stupid."

"Damn right it was stupid and it almost cost

me my life." Angel frowned.

"Now you see why I was begging for your forgiveness. This shit is all my fault, but I tried to make it right."

"What do you mean?"

"After I knew my men had got you back Nico called me."

"What did he say?" Angel was curious to know.

"I told him I was willing to pay the money that I owed him and we could call it even, but he declined. He said he didn't want the money.

"Then what did he want?"

"You."

"What!" Angel was shocked by what Darien said. "You must've misunderstood him."

"No, I didn't. He made it very clear that I could keep the money, all he wanted was you. Angel, did something happen between the two of you while you were held hostage? You can tell me, baby. I wouldn't blame you. It wouldn't have been your fault."

"You mean something like sex?"

"Yes."

"You know, when I first woke up and I was in bed and he was sitting in a chair looking at me; for a quick second I thought maybe he had tried to take advantage of me, but by the disgusting look on his face when I asked I knew he hadn't. He didn't seem attracted to me at all... I mean I am young enough to be his daughter."

"A lot of older men date and even marry younger women so that don't mean shit."

"True, but I didn't get that vibe from him. He was actually pretty nice to me," Angel acknowledged thinking back to their conversations.

"Don't be fooled by that nigga's charms. He one of those smooth talkin' New York cats. He want you back for a reason. He up to something. Nico Carter is a dangerous man and I don't want you anywhere near him. I've already made arrangements for us to get out of here."

"Where are we going?"

"Vegas."

"To live?"

"Yes, at least for a little while. I have to train for an upcoming fight anyway. We'll be staying at a penthouse with round the clock security. Nobody will be able to get to you."

"But I have a business to run. I have a lot of girls that depend on me. I'm sure many of them haven't been able to work since I've been gone."

"You can run your business right from Vegas." Angel thought about what Darien said and he did have a point. To run her business all she really required was a phone, computer, and an account for money to be deposited.

"Okay, so when are we leaving?"

"Right now. I have a private jet waiting for us."

"Wow, well I need to make one stop on our way to the airport."

"No problem, but we need to go. I'm sure Nico's men are plotting on how to get through these gates at this very moment so we have no time to waste."

Angel grabbed a few things from her closet and bathroom before heading out. "Vegas here I come."

Chapter Six

Quiet Storm

When Taren opened her front door she thought she was looking at a ghost. She could barely hide her shock, but she tried.

"Omigosh! Angel, I was so worried about you. Where have you been?" Taren reached out and pulled Angel in for a long embrace.

"I was worried about you, too. Darien said he spoke to you briefly when I first went missing, but I still had to make sure you were okay. I can only stay for a second, can I come in?"

"Of course! Can I get you anything?" Taren offered.

"No, I'm good." Angel sat down on the couch. "Darien is outside in the car waiting for me. I had him stop by here on our way to the airport."

"Airport... where are you going?"

"I'm not allowed to say. I know you're my best friend I should at least be able to tell you, but Darien made me promise not to tell anybody until he said it was okay. After what happened to me, he's not taking any chances."

"That's understandable. So what did happen? I saw you coming my way and I waved my arm and I thought you saw me."

"Yeah, I did." Angel nodded.

"But then I waited thinking you were circling back around, but you never showed up. It was like you vanished. I waited for a while and then called you, but didn't get an answer. When the tow truck showed up a few minutes later the man was able to get my car started so I went home. My phone died so I wasn't able to call you again until I got back to my apartment. But when I did call still no answer. I didn't know what was going on. It wasn't until Darien called me looking for you that I realized something was wrong."

"Girl, the shit was crazy. A car came out of nowhere and was blocking my way down the street. So I did a U-turn to go down a back street and then that same car blocked me from the back and a black van was blocking me in the front. I blew my horn then rolled my window to tell the van to move. Next thing I knew I was getting pulled out my car and thrown in the back of the van. It was craziness that seemed to go down in a matter of seconds." Angel was shaking her head recalling how everything went down.

"Are you serious! Who would do something like that and why?" Taren questioned as if she didn't already know.

"I can't get into all that right now, but it has to do with Darien so we're getting out of town until things cool down."

"How long will you be gone?"

"Not sure, but I plan on running the business from where I'm at so the girls will be straight. I'm making deposits in everybody's account to make up for the time I was out of commission. I brought your money with me since I knew I would see you before I left," Angel said handing Taren an envelope of cash.

"You didn't have to do this." Taren smiled,

overjoyed to get the cash.

"I wanted to. How are the girls? I haven't had a chance to call any of them yet. I'll be sending out emails to everyone, which will include my new cell phone number. How is Laurie? I really need to check on her."

"I've spoken to Laurie a few times. She seems to be doing much better. She even mentioned coming back to work."

"Really? Even after what happened to her she wants to come back to work?"

"That's what she said."

"I still haven't found out who is responsible for beating her like that, but I will. When I do, they will pay dearly. Well, I better be going. I told Darien I would only be in here for a few minutes. Of course when I get to chatting with my best friend a few minutes can easily turn into a few hours." Angel laughed.

"You ain't lying, girl! I'm just glad to see that you're okay. You had me scared. I don't know what I would do if something happened to you." Taren gave a fake warm smile that appeared to be sincere.

"I'll be in touch soon. Love you, girl." Angel gave Taren a goodbye hug and a kiss on the cheek before leaving.

"Love you, too." Taren waved as Angel got in the car. She continued to wave as they drove off. "I can't believe that bitch is not only alive, but walking around free as a bird!" Taren snapped before slamming the front door. She then reached for her cell phone ready to unleash her anger.

"I told you not to fuckin' call me!" Tony barked when he answered his phone. "Yo' dumbass the one that got me jammed up now."

"Oh really motherfucker! You could've told me that Angel was no longer being held hostage. I almost shitted on myself when I opened my door and she was standing there," Taren cracked.

"You saw Angel... when?" In a flash Tony's tone went from angry and dismissive to sugary sweet. "I apologize for snapping at you, Taren. I have a lot of pressure on me. This Angel situation got everybody on edge. So tell me when did you see her?"

"Nigga, fuck you! I ain't telling you shit!" Taren spit then ended the call. She reached over to the end table and pulled out a Newport. She lit it and leaned back in the chair. She crossed her legs, rocking back and forth trying to figure out what her next move would be. Taren felt Tony had become dead weight and wasn't doing a damn thing to help her cause. She got up, went to the kitchen, and got a bottle of wine from the refrigerator. Taren decided to finish the entire bottle, go to sleep, wake up in the morning, and devise a new plan to finally bring Angel down for good, since no one else seemed capable of getting the job done but her.

At least twenty of Nico's men stormed into Darien Blaze's mansion in all black everything with guns aimed. They were ready to shoot to kill anybody that stood between them and getting Angel back. After sifting through every inch of the property it was evident that if Angel had been there she was long gone.

"Boss, Angel isn't here... nobody is," Elijah told Nico.

"Did they leave any clues as to where they might have went?"

"Nothing. It looks like they left in a hurry."

"Darien can only hide Angel for so long. We'll find them. I'm boarding my flight to New York. I'll be gone for a few days, but you keep me informed of any new developments. Finding Angel is your top priority. I'll be in touch."

When Nico took his seat on the plane, his mind took him back to many years ago. To the time he was on the run and had met Lisa, Angel's mother. He remembered how sweet, innocent, and beautiful she was. Much too innocent for him and the life he lived. But instead of letting her go, Nico kept Lisa in his world until she finally had enough.

Damn Lisa, you hated me to the point you felt it was better to lie and tell me you had an abortion instead of letting me be a part of our child's life. I'm trying to understand what you were thinking. How you thought depriving our daughter of her father was the best thing for her. Maybe if you hadn't died after giving birth, you would've changed your mind, but now I'll never know. What I do know is you blessed me with a beautiful daughter and I will do whatever is necessary to have a relationship with her. I've missed out on so much of her life, but I'll spend the rest of mine trying to make up for lost time, Nico promised himself as the plane took off.

Chapter Seven

Welcome To Vegas

From the moment they stepped off the private jet and were whisked away to their hotel suite, Angel was in awe of Las Vegas. This was her first visit to the colorful oasis and she looked forward to staying for a while.

The private elevator led them to a 12-room suite that took up the entire floor of the hotel. The only way to describe it was shameless glamour.

From the grand foyer entrance with an elaborate floor made of four kinds of marble, to the opulent crystal chandeliers, gold sofas, and cushions with fabrics woven with platinum and gold. Ivory, gold leaf, frescoes, heated flooring, and stained glass lead to floor-to-ceiling windows with an elaborate wrap around terrace, which included a swimming pool and jacuzzi overlooking a view of the strip. There were three master bedrooms that each included an oversized marble bathroom, steam room, sauna, individual rain shower booth, walk-in dressing room, and of course Frette linen sheets. With an indoor waterfall, Steinway grand piano, private cinema, fitness center, butler, and chef there was absolutely no reason to leave the suite.

"I'm almost speechless. I've seen some incredible homes, I mean we live in one, but I've never seen anything like this. Talk about no holds barred luxury." Angel gasped.

"You know what the best part is," Darien stated.

"Besides the huge vases of pink roses that are perfuming the air?" Angel smiled.

"So you know that was all me," Darien boasted. "I personally requested for those to be here because I thought they added a feminine touch that you would appreciate. I was afraid you wouldn't notice with so much extravagance going on in here."

"I definitely noticed and I appreciate the gesture. Now, getting back to the other best part." Angel laughed.

"The best part is the bulletproof doors and windows. This is what the hotel describes as the perfect safe house suite for the privacy conscious celebs, oh and paranoid." Darien chuckled.

"So we're safer than safe here." Angel joked.

"We better be. But just to be sure, I have my own round the clock security team here and I'm also utilizing the hotel's security."

"There is more than enough space to have an entire army stay here," Angel commented looking around the sprawling suite.

"I also made sure they set up your own private office so you could run your business."

"You did! Thank you, baby." Angel gave Darien a long hug and kiss. "That was so sweet of you, especially since I know you would prefer me giving up my escort business."

"Babe, I just feel there is so much more you can do then sell pussy to rich niggas."

"How soon we forget that you were one of those rich niggas."

"That don't count. I was only trying to hook up with you. Plus, I didn't touch none of those chicks just my boys. I put that on everything."

"I know. I checked with my girls before I agreed to go out on a date with you." Angel winked.

"I should've known wit' yo' slick ass." Darien laughed, wrapping his arms around Angel's waist and lifting her up. He carried her up the winding, gold-encrusted staircase locking lips the entire way. Darien and Angel were completely engrossed with their passionate kisses that they almost walked past the first bedroom. Darien back peddled still holding on tightly to Angel's waist with her legs wrapped around him.

"Damn, I've missed being inside of you," Darien whispered in Angel's ears before laying her down on the bed.

"I've missed you, too." Angel stared in Darien's eyes as he undressed her. When he took off his shirt and jeans she was amazed by the cut of his physique. During those days they were apart and all the craziness that took place, Angel had almost forgotten how perfectly chiseled her man was. Darien took his time sprinkling kisses on her inner thighs before taking the tip of his tongue and gently licking Angel's wet clit. Those gentle licks soon turned to Darien filling his entire mouth with Angel's sweet juices. Her sighs of pleasure got him even more aroused as the balls of his fingers rubbed her hardened nipples. His rock hard dick entered Angel causing her to scream out, pressing her nails deep into Darien's back. With every thrust, Angel's cries of pleasure became louder and louder as she welcomed the pain of him filling up the insides of her warmth.

"I love you so much," Darien said between purposeful strokes.

"I love you, too," Angel purred as she pulled him closer. "I never want to let you go."

"You never have to. We belong together... forever."

Darien's words rang like soothing music in Angel's ears. As the two made love, the moonlight seemed to create a glow around their naked bodies, with their souls becoming one in the magical Vegas night.

Chapter Eight

Hood Politics

"My man, Nico! I was beginning to think you were never coming back from Miami," Genesis cracked when he opened the door and let Nico inside his condo.

"What can I say, I got caught up in the warm weather and beaches."

"Yeah right. You were born and raised in New York. You wouldn't know how to live without cold weather and snow," Genesis joked. "But seriously, I was getting a little concerned. With Aaliyah still missing and business being shaky I figured you would want to be here. Not saying you can't conduct business in Miami but..."

"I know what you saying," Nico interrupted. "Originally I went to Miami to handle the Blaze situation."

"Right... right," Genesis nodded, while pouring himself and Nico a drink.

"But while dealing with him there were some new developments."

"New developments like what?" Genesis questioned.

Nico hesitated for a moment before answering. He wanted to keep the identity of Angel hidden for a while to protect her, but Genesis was his business partner and he considered him to be a valued friend. If there was anyone he could trust with the information, he knew it was Genesis. Plus, Nico was ready to share the news with someone.

"I have another daughter," Nico stated casually, taking a seat on the sofa.

"I'm sorry, say that again," Genesis said, handing him a drink. "I don't think I heard you correctly.

"Yes, you did. I have a daughter. Her name is Angel."

"Wow, when will I be able to meet Angel?"

"Soon I hope, but it's complicated."

"I'm sure you don't share all of your personal relationships with me. But in recent years I've never heard you mention any woman that you were serious enough with where you all would've conceived a child or was this something unexpected?" Genesis asked.

"Do you remember Lisa? You never met her, but I mentioned her a few times to you."

"Yes, you dated her years ago. I remember how angry you were when she got an abortion... wait," Genesis hesitated for a second as if putting the pieces of the puzzle together. "Is Angel the child Lisa said she aborted?"

"Yes," Nico acknowledged putting his head down. "I'm still trying to wrap my head around why Lisa would keep me away from my child."

"Did you ask her?"

"I can't. She's dead."

"What!"

"From what I understand, she died in the hospital after giving birth to Angel. Her mother raised our daughter, but no one knew I was the father."

"I'm sorry, man. That's got to be a hard pill to swallow."

"What's even harder is that once I got the paternity test confirming Angel is mine, I can't find her. Even if I'm able to, I don't know how accepting she's going to be," Nico admitted, finishing his drink.

"I guess this is more of the complicated part."

"Damn sure is. She's Blaze's girlfriend," Nico revealed.

"You weren't lying when you said it was complicated. She's the girlfriend of one of our enemies. That ain't good. Tell me more." Genesis sat back and listened intently to the long version of what went down with Nico, Angel, and Blaze. He got an earful, much more than what he expected. By the time Nico finished giving him the details surrounding the discovery of his daughter, Genesis needed another drink.

"I have two daughters and both of them are missing. It makes me question is this some sort of karma for all the fucked up things I've done in my life."

"I asked myself the same question when Talisa died in my arms on our wedding day and I had to raise our son alone. On the flip side, our son survived that shooting and now Amir is an exceptional young man. The point I'm trying to make is that yeah, we've done a lot of bad, but out of that we've also done a lot of good. If you want to beat yourself up, then with the other hand you should pat yourself on the back."

"I hear what you're saying, Genesis, but if I don't find Aaliyah and Angel none of that matters."

"You will find them. Aaliyah is a fighter. Wherever she is, she's raising hell and figuring out a way to get the fuck outta there. I don't know Angel but she has your DNA running through her blood, so I wouldn't worry about her either. I'm sure she knows how to take care of herself."

"For the sake of my sanity, I'ma go 'head and believe what you're saying to be the truth. So we're going to table this topic for now. Let's get to this new information you uncovered," Nico said rubbing his hands together.

"I can't take credit for uncovering it."

"Then who?"

"Our other partner that you prefer not to acknowledge... Lorenzo," Genesis smirked.

"And here I thought nothing else could ruin my day." Nico shook his head.

"You'll never admit it, but I think deep down inside you actually like Lorenzo," Genesis joked, fucking with Nico.

"Man, if you don't cut that bullshit out and tell me what he found out..."

"We finally got the confirmation we needed. Arnez is alive and he is responsible for the shooting at the warehouse and at your wedding with Precious." Genesis regretted saying that last part the moment it slipped out of his mouth.

"Yo, you determined to fuck up my day... huh? Now I need you to pour me another drink," Nico huffed.

"I apologize. I know the wound is still fresh."

"No need to apologize. It ain't your fault Precious got her memory back. Let's table that topic too. Back to Arnez. Now that we know he is alive and well, where is he?"

"Underground, but I reached out to Renny. If anybody can pull him out of hiding, it's him."

"The cousin that shot and left him for dead. I seriously doubt that."

"Don't underestimate Renny. I'm sure he knows Arnez and the way he operates better than anybody."

"Do you think he'll be willing to help?"

"All this shit is street politics. With the right motivation, I'm counting on Renny giving us all the help we need," Genesis said confidently.

Chapter Nine

Excuse Me Miss

Angel decided to browse through some of the upscale boutiques in the hotel lobby, after Darien informed her he had planned a romantic dinner for the two of them that night. They had been in such a rush to leave Miami that Angel had forgotten to pack any dressy clothes, but she welcomed the opportunity to shop for something new.

"Can I help you find something, Miss?" the

sales clerk asked Angel when she came inside the store.

"For now I'm just looking, but if I find something I like, I'll let you know." Angel smiled. She spotted a few cute dresses and a jumper that she wanted to try on. Angel grabbed them off the racks and headed towards the dressing rooms. She decided to try on the white Balmain first. It was an unapologetically sexy cutaway jumper she knew would have Darien unable to concentrate on his dinner because he would be too busy lusting after her.

"You have to get that. It looks super hot on you," a girl commented when Angel stepped out her dressing room to get a better look at herself in the bigger mirrors.

"Thanks. I do love it." Angel grinned, turning around to see how it fit her from every angle. "That dress you have on looks hot on you, too," Angel said noticing the girl's figure looked perfect in the red stunner. The dress had a flamenco feel to it and she was able to pull it off.

"Doesn't it," the girl agreed. "I'm wearing it tonight. I can't wait!"

"Sounds like you have some major plans."

"I do or at least I hope so. But I think wearing this dress should seal any deal." The girl winked at Angel before disappearing back into her dressing room.

Angel giggled at the bubbly girl. Her upbeat attitude reminded Angel of Laurie. *Gosh, I need to call Laurie. Make sure she's doing okay. She's the only one that hasn't responded to the email blast I sent out to all the girls. Taren did say that Laurie mentioned she was ready to get back to work so I assumed I would've heard back from her. I'm definitely going to call her tomorrow,* Angel thought to herself as she tried on the last dress before taking the one she wanted and the jumper to the register to check out.

"I'm sorry this credit card has been declined," Angel heard the clerk telling the girl she was just talking to.

"Are you sure?"

"Yes, I ran it twice," the lady said, handing the credit card back to the girl.

"Here, try this one." The girl fumbled through her wallet before handing the sales clerk another Visa.

"Sorry, this one is no good either," the clerk smirked.

The girl continued fumbling through her wallet and then pulled out a few twenty-dollar bills that probably couldn't buy her a pair of pantyhose at the store.

"She's with me. I'll pay for it," Angel spoke up and said. The girl turned around with wide eyes to see who was playing secret Santa. Angel gave her a slight smile and then stepped forward to pay for the items. "I'll be paying cash."

The clerk grinned, more than happy to take the money from Angel's hand.

"Why did you do that for me?" the girl blurted out once her and Angel walked out the store.

"Honestly, because you remind me of a girl I know. You all look nothing alike, but you have the same cheery personality. So when I saw you in your little bind, I wanted to help."

"Thank you so so much! I seriously appreciate you bailing me out of that jam. I was mortified when both my cards got declined."

"It happens to the best of us."

"Well, I'm going to pay you back every dime."

"You don't have to do that," Angel insisted.

"I want to. Plus, after tonight I'm gonna make a killing. I'll have more than enough to pay you back."

"Wait... are you a working girl?"

"I like to describe myself as a delicious dessert that men pay to get a taste of so yeah I'm a working girl."

Angel burst out laughing. "You really are funny. So do you work for an escort service?"

"No. When I lived in New York the escort service I worked for took so much of my money and I hated the men they set me up with. One guy was so unattractive, so sloppy and huge I thought I was gonna puke. I refused to have sex with him. So I decided when I came to Vegas I would try my luck selecting my own men."

"How's that been working for you?"

"It has its pros and its cons. I mean, I've had some men that have totally screwed me, like literally out of my money and I've had some others that have been straight shooters. It really depends on where you meet the guys. Like tonight one of my friends told me about this super exclusive party this man is having at the hotel. There should be so much money up in there. I'll easily make some cash and get future clients too," the girl bragged.

"I didn't catch your name," Angel said, very intrigued by what the girl was saying.

"Heather, that's my real name but Amber is my working my name."

"Which do you prefer for me to call you?"

"Amber."

"Amber, I'm Angel. Nice to meet you," she

said shaking her hand. "What if I told you, I can guarantee you'll make so much money, that your credit cards will never be denied again."

"I would say I'm listening."

"But here's the thing. I don't want you working that party tonight."

"Why not? I really need the money. Not only do I have to pay you back, but baby I got bills!"

"I'm sure you do. Clearly you have very expensive taste." Angel laughed, eyeing the dress she just purchased for Amber.

"If you want to attract money you have to look like money," Amber reasoned.

"I couldn't agree with you more. Although you seem to be rather young, you have a very polished look to you," Angel said sizing up the tall, slender brown beauty. She wore her brown hair, which appeared to be professionally highlighted, back in a sleek bun with very natural makeup that gave her a supermodel look.

"Most people think I'm nineteen, but I'm actually twenty-three. Yes, I'm still young, but not teenage young. You still haven't told me why you don't want me to work that party tonight."

"Because I want you to work for me. I run an escort service called Angel's Girls."

"Really! Wow... you look too young to run

your own business. How exciting. Would I be one of your first girls," Amber beamed.

"Actually, I've been running a very successful business for sometime now. I've relocated temporarily from Miami to Vegas. So although you're not my first girl overall, you are my first girl in Vegas."

"Great!" Amber clapped her hands.

"The reason I don't want you to work that party tonight is because I think it's beneath you. I have an extensive clientele list and I can have you working immediately. I don't want one of my girls at some party looking thirsty. That sort of defeats the purpose of putting on a thousand dollar dress, don't you think?" Angel frowned.

"You do have a point."

"Of course I do. If you decide to come work with me, I'll always give you the best points or better yet pointers. What do you say, Amber?"

"You for sure seem to have your shit together. I mean you did pay for my dress. I would be a fool to turn you down."

"Good decision. Here," Angel said, retrieving some money from her purse. "This should hold you over until I get you working."

"You really are amazing. Luck must really be on my side today."

"If you play your cards right, your luck will only get better. Here, take my number and call me tomorrow. I get all my girls tested and I run a criminal background check before I put them to work."

"No problem. I'm super clean in both areas."

"Perfect. I normally like for my girls to take an etiquette class also, but I think you might be able to skip that part. You have excellent taste in clothes and you're very put together. So call me tomorrow."

"I'm so excited. I'll try not to call you too early."

"That's a good idea."

"You know my friend, the one who told me about the party tonight and who is also my roommate."

"What about her?"

"I think she would be an excellent Angel's girl too. She's even more polished than me."

"When you come by tomorrow, bring her."

"Awesome! Thanks again, Angel. I'm going to be your best girl yet." Amber gave Angel her signature wink and headed off with the biggest smile on her face.

Angel was smiling too, but for a different reason. She had recruited her first girl in Vegas and she appeared to be a winner. If her friend was a taker then that would make two. Angel got such a rush running her escort company and she began thinking how lucrative it would be if she had girls in all the major cities. Eventually maybe even taking her business international. Ideas began to run rampant in her mind. She couldn't help herself. By nature Angel was a hustler.

Chapter Ten

Girls Wanna Have Fun

"Girl, Angel is a boss bitch foreal! I mean she off in another city and state, but holding shit down here in Miami. I'm still making money like she never left. When we first all had that conference call and she said business was going to flow like usual, I'm not gonna lie, I was looking at the phone sideways. I was like there is no way Angel is going to be able to pull this off, no matter how good her intentions were. But that bad bitch proved me wrong and I'm glad she did," Aspen cheered.

Taren was rolling her eyes on the low as she picked up the remote control and began turning the channel. "So what do you want to eat for lunch?"

"What are you talking about, Taren? We just ate." Aspen raised her eyebrow. "You can't be hungry again already? Let me find out you pregnant."

"Heifer, ain't nobody pregnant," Taren mumbled. "I was trying to get you to shut the fuck up and that was the first thing that popped in my head."

"Why you been so grouchy lately?" Aspen folded her arms and stared at Taren waiting for her response. "I know what it is... you missing your best friend Angel. She'll be back, girl. So stop worrying." Aspen nudged Taren's arm.

"You so clueless," Taren muttered under her breath. Aspen had no idea why Taren was annoyed and it had nothing to do with her worrying about Angel. Taren was in a funk because since Angel left she had been spending all her time trying to find her exact location, but she couldn't find squat. Angel had vanished and it was driving Taren crazy.

"Neither one of us has to work tonight, why don't we go out and have some fun. We can even invite Laurie. The three of us haven't been out together since she was in the hospital."

"That would be straight. I'm tired of thinking about bullshit anyway. Going out and having some fun might take the edge off."

"Do you think we can get Laurie to come too?"

"I'm not sure. Her moods go up and down. A few weeks ago she told me she was ready to go back to work. Then she changed her mind." Taren shrugged.

"Can you blame her? I mean, you saw Laurie in the hospital. The way that man beat her." Aspen shook her head, having flashbacks to that night at the hospital. "Because of what happened to Laurie, I carry a gun in my purse every time I meet with a client. I'm not taking any chances."

"Damn, Aspen. I never pictured you as the type to carry a gun. You seem too nervous and scared."

"That's the reason I do carry a gun because I am scared. I would shoot and run!" she laughed.

"You are so silly. I can see you now, shooting and running."

"Yep, but at least I'll be alive and not in the same fucked up condition that monster left Laurie. Let me text her right now. I hope she does come out with us. I miss her."

"I miss her, too," Taren chimed in.

"OMG! She just texted me back and said she would love to hang tonight."

"Seriously? I didn't think she would."

"Me neither, but maybe she's ready to put that incident behind her and start living her life again. It will take time, but it's all about baby steps and I think Laurie is about to take hers." Aspen hoped she was right.

"We 'bout to get in some trouble tonight, girl. It's time to party, party, and party some more!" Taren shouted before slapping hands with Aspen.

"Baily, I have the best news," Amber hollered when she got back to her apartment.

"Can you keep your voice down? Don't you see me meditating," Baily snapped in a low voice. She closed her eyes so she could focus on being calm and composed.

"That lil' yoga you're doing can wait!" Amber retorted, walking over to turn off the soothing noise of the ocean coming from the sound machine.

"Did you really cut that off? You know how much that relaxes me when I'm doing my meditation. Turn it back on... now."

Normally Amber would give into Baily's request, because this was a daily ritual for her roommate, but business trumped all that.

"You can get back to what you were doing, after I tell you the good news.

"Hurry up! I have to get in the shower soon to get ready for that party tonight. You need to start getting dressed too, because I know you're not wearing what you have on," Baily smacked. Although Amber looked sexy and sophisticated in her high waist jeans, cropped silk blouse and pumps, Baily was positive her friend would never go to an exclusive upscale party wearing it.

"Duh! Of course I'm not wearing this, but I won't be wearing anything."

"I'm all for being bold, but you can't be planning on going to that party naked." Baily was concerned and baffled by what Amber said.

"Don't be silly, Baily," Amber rolled her eyes. "What I was trying to tell you was I'm not attending the party and neither are you."

"Unless you hit the lottery after you left this apartment this morning, yes you will be going to that party. Did you not see all those bills stacked up on the kitchen counter?"

"Yeah, I saw them."

"They're not going to pay themselves. We need some money and that party is going to make that happen," Baily huffed, anxious to get back to meditating. "Now turn my sound back on!"

"Can you just listen to me for a second before shutting me down. You have no idea what I'm about to tell you."

"Five minutes, Amber. I'm setting the timer on my iPhone so use your time wisely."

"I met a girl today named Angel and she wants to sign me to her escort service. I told her about you too and we're meeting her tomorrow. And get this, she said I'm going to make so much money that my credit cards will never be declined again," Amber gushed.

"You don't know anything about this girl and even if you did, she could put you to work and keep all the cash."

"I doubt it. Look at this thousand dollar

dress she bought me after my credit card was declined." Amber pulled out the red stunner that had her looking like a runway model.

"Nice dress, but I ain't impressed," Baily shot back.

"Then maybe this will impress you." Amber pulled out the cash Angel gave her.

Baily's mouth dropped. "Where did you get all that money?"

"I take it you're impressed now," Amber giggled.

Baily adjusted the strap on her peach sports bra before standing up and walking towards Amber. She unraveled her loose bun letting her dark auburn curls fall past her shoulders. She stood in front of Amber as the sweat glistened on her body emphasizing her toned abs. She used a towel to wipe herself off and then gulped down half a bottle of water.

"Yes, I'm impressed," Baily finally said before finishing off the remaining water.

"I knew you would be! But like I was telling you, she doesn't want us going to that party tonight. She said it would make me look thirsty and that would defeat the purpose of wearing a thousand dollar dress to a party."

"She has a point."

"That's the same thing I said!" Amber sounded extra giddy.

"But does this Angel chick realize how broke you are?"

"I explained my situation to her and that's why she gave me the cash. She likes to have her girls tested for STDs and run a background check before putting them to work. So I'm meeting her tomorrow and she said I could bring you with me."

Baily raised an eyebrow believing this all sounded too good to be true. But based on the information Amber was giving her it seemed worthy of a meeting.

"I'm game. Let's just hope this Angel woman is the real deal. This is Vegas and scams are the norm."

"I can understand your skepticism, but once you meet her all of your cynicism will vanish," Amber promised.

Baily held up her hands and said, "Fingers crossed hoping you're right. And since no party tonight, I guess we'll be ordering pizza and watching a movie.

"Fuck that! We may not be going to that party, but no sense in staying in this cramped apartment when we got more than enough cash to have some fun. Go take a shower and get dressed. We're going out tonight!"

"You got it! Time to get turnt up in Vegas!" Baily beamed.

Chapter Eleven

Blood On My Hands

"Laurie, I can't believe we finally got you out the house, especially after you bailed on us last week," Aspen cracked.

"She bailed at the very last minute, too," Taren added, pressing down on the breaks suddenly, after getting caught by a red light.

"I know. I felt bad about that, but I was in a fucked up mood so I wouldn't have been any fun,"

Laurie explained.

"We forgive you, but we in the no fucked up zone tonight. We leaving the misery behind and only focusing on having fun! Deal?" Aspen asked directing her question to Laurie.

"I'll try my best just as long as we don't run into any fools tonight."

"I'm prepared if we do," Aspen said, holding up her purse.

"What you got some mace in there?" Laurie questioned.

"Something even better... a gun. I got this motherfucker hot off the streets which means it ain't registered. So if we need to use it, it can't be traced back to us," Aspen bragged.

"Bitch, you is a fool!" Taren joked. "You better be happy we going to a lounge or you would have to leave that shit in the car."

"Aspen, when did you start carrying a gun.... nevermind, don't answer that. I just need you to get me one, too."

"You serious, Laurie? Because if you are say the word and I'm on it."

"I'm very serious especially since I think I'm finally ready to get back to work."

"Here we go again," Taren mocked, staring at Laurie in the backseat.

"I wasn't ready before, but I am now. I actually spoke to Angel yesterday and she's been so patient and understanding. She said she would start lining up clients for me."

"Angel should be patient and understanding since it's her fault you ended up in the hospital," Taren remarked

"You can't blame Angel, Taren. She is thorough with vetting potential clients. Sometimes people slip through the cracks," Aspen reasoned.

"Clearly she's not thorough enough. Angel is my best friend and I love her, but wrong is wrong. If she had been more careful none of this would've happened to Laurie."

For the duration of the car ride it was complete silence. Taren accomplished what she set out to do, cause doubt amongst the girls. Neither Laurie nor Aspen wanted to admit it, but Taren knew both of them felt she had valid points even if her point had no merit. Taren was still scheming on how to bring Angel down starting with her business since killing her was out of reach at the moment. Taren figured she would start taking advantage of Angel being in another state by planting seeds of doubts in each girl working for her. She was subtle, but continued to whisper negative thoughts about Angel to each of them. Taren hadn't given up on her goal of starting her own escort business, taking Angel's clients and girls with her.

When Taren, Aspen, and Laurie arrived at the artsy décor lounge on NW 23rd St., after being escorted to a table, they immediately ordered the hookah flavor to pair with their drinks. The DJ had the perfect music coming through the speakers that put you in a feel good mood.

"This place is amazeballs," Laurie smirked, dancing to the music in her seat.

"Aren't you happy you came." Aspen stated, moving her body to the music too.

"I'll be right back," Taren said standing up. "I have to go to the restroom."

Laurie and Aspen were hardly paying attention to what Taren said because as she was leaving, the waitress brought their drinks, wings, and hookah flavor.

"Why the fuck haven't you been answering my calls and text messages!" the boisterous voice startled Taren as she was about to open the bathroom door. The heavy hand yanked her arm, almost spinning her around.

"Nigga, is you crazy!" Taren barked when her eyes met Tony's. "Who the fuck you think you grabbing on."

"Don't get brand new on me because we out in public. I'll jam yo' ass up right in this motherfucker," Tony barked back.

"Oh really? You don't want it wit' me, Tony. Ain't nobody scared of yo' big ass."

"As many secrets as we share, you should be," Tony countered.

"The secrets work both ways. So what do you want, Tony?"

"I want you to tell me where Angel is."

"With all that money and security Nico Carter has he still can't locate Angel," Taren said sarcastically. "I don't know what to tell you 'cause I don't know where homegirl is either. Now if you'll excuse me, I need to use the restroom."

"We're not done yet!" Tony snarled, this time grabbing Taren's arm even tighter.

"When the waitress gets back order me another drink because now I need to use the restroom," Laurie told Aspen.

"Will do. I wonder what's taking Taren so

long," Aspen wondered.

"Who knows, there might be a line, but I hope not because I need to go." Laurie rushed to the restroom, but quickly froze mid-step as she got closer. People kept bumping into Laurie as they passed her by, but that still wasn't enough to bring her out of a daze. It wasn't until someone bumped Laurie so hard and knocked her purse to the floor, that she snapped out of her trance. Instead of continuing to the bathroom she ran back to where Aspen was sitting.

"You got back super fast," Aspen commented when Laurie sat down. "So what's taking Taren so long... did you see her in the restroom?"

Laurie didn't answer Aspen. Instead, she quickly gulped down her drink then reached over and grabbed Taren's before gulping that down too. Laurie extended her arm to take Aspen's drink, but wasn't quick enough because Aspen picked it up first.

"What is wrong with Taren and why are you shaking like that?" Laurie's strange behavior had Aspen perplexed and worried. "Laurie will you please answer me? You're scaring me!"

"I saw him." That was all Laurie managed to get out as her voice quivered.

"Who is him?" Laurie's shaking hadn't let up

and Aspen began searching around the lounge for Taren, needing her help. "Where the fuck are you, Taren!" she shouted out loud becoming frustrated. Aspen then sent out a 911 text to her friend hoping that would make her reappear.

"The man who beat me up and put me in the hospital is here."

When Aspen heard those words leave Laurie's mouth she did a double take. "You saw the man that assaulted you here at this lounge?"

"Yes," Laurie answered softly as her shaking continued. She almost dropped her glass of water, but Aspen held it up for her.

"Where is he?" Aspen questioned while continuing to hold up the glass of water for Laurie. Once she took her last sip, Laurie appeared to calm down. The shaking stopped and now there was only a slight trembling. "Are you okay?"

"He's here. The monster who put me in the hospital is here and I saw him talking to Taren in front of the restroom."

"Talking to Taren! Stay here, I'll be right back!" Right when Aspen was getting up from her chair, Taren showed up. "Who is the guy you were talking to and where is he?" Aspen blurted.

"What guy and what's wrong with Laurie? She looks like she's seen a ghost."

"She did! She saw you talking to the man that assaulted her."

Taren's eyes darted around before landing back on Aspen. She then shot Laurie a stare. "Oh you must be talking about that guy that was trying to hit on me when I was on my way into the restroom. I don't know who that is. That's the first time I've ever seen him. Laurie, are you sure that's the man that assaulted you?"

"I'm positive." Laurie confirmed.

"Laurie, you stay here. Come on, Taren. I want you to show me who the guy is." Aspen grabbed Taren's hand and the ladies hurried off.

Aspen was pulling Taren around every inch of the lounge in search of the mystery man. Taren had seen Tony once, but didn't point him out. Taren wanted no part of the situation and so she pretended not to see him. After twenty minutes without a sighting, Aspen and Taren went back to the table.

"Where the hell did Laurie go?" Aspen gasped.

"I don't know. Maybe she went to the restroom." Taren shrugged.

"Oh gosh." Aspen put her hand over her mouth.

"What's wrong?"

"My purse. My purse is gone," Aspen revealed becoming panic-stricken.

"Do you think Laurie took it?" Taren asked.

"If she did then that means Laurie has my gun." Aspen shook her head. The idea of Laurie walking around in her fragile condition with a loaded gun had Aspen about to hyperventilate.

Chapter Twelve

Don't Come For Me And I Won't Come For You

"Ladies, I apologize for the delay meeting with you, but things have been a tad hectic for me," Angel explained after Amber and Baily sat down and got comfortable.

Angel was telling the truth. For the last week or so she put all her time and attention getting her girls in Miami back on rotation. They had been without while Nico was holding her captive and she wanted to make sure they were straight before getting her Vegas girls in check. Although Angel had to postpone meeting with Amber and Baily in person, she did have them tested and had a criminal background check done.

"I'm happy to report that both of you girls came back clean as a whistle." Angel smiled.

"I told you we would." Amber winked.

"Yes, you did. Hopefully you'll maintain the same level of honesty as we continue to work together," Angel added. "So, now that we got that out the way let's talk about getting you ladies working."

"Wonderful!" both Amber and Baily said in unison.

"I give all my girls a shopping budget when they first start working, so they can wear the appropriate attire on the job." The ladies eyes both widened in excitement after Angel informed them of that. "This should be enough." Angel stood up and handed both of them an envelope of money.

"Thank you." They both grinned.

"I need to see everything you all pick out to make sure I find it acceptable."

"Of course, that's not a problem," Baily spoke up and said, while Amber nodded in agreement.

"But I'm not worried. Based on the dress Amber picked out from the hotel boutique and the way you ladies are dressed today, I'm almost positive I'll approve.

Angel was impressed by both Amber's and Baily's choice of fashion and their style in general. Amber had her back in the same sleek bun with cream slacks; a cream fitted tank top with gold accessories and nude open toe high heel sandals. Her friend Baily was equally stunning with her auburn curls cascading past her shoulders with a deep side part. She was wearing a simple yet sexy taupe colored wrap dress with matching colored pumps. Her jewelry was minimal with just a pair of diamond-studded earrings.

"We've already discussed money and I'm sure you all have read over the pamphlet that details the rules if you want to continue to be part of my organization."

"Yes," they both acknowledged. Angel tried to conduct her business as any other organization. If you read the pamphlet and paperwork all the girls had to read and sign, it seemed like Angel's

Girls catered to models and actresses instead of being a high-end escort service.

"Great, so then do either of you have any other questions?"

"When do we start?" Amber and Baily wanted to know.

"Friday. I will give you all the details tomorrow. I will tell you they are professional athletes, who are friends in town for the weekend, so you ladies will be working together."

"That's awesome!" they both seemed excited.

"I have another question," Baily said, raising her hand.

"What is it?"

"I know a couple of other girls that would definitely be interested working for your organization. But I wanted to see if you were still accepting new girls?"

"If I think they are a good fit then yes. Have them email me their pic with the same online application you ladies filled out and we'll go from there."

"Thank you so much, Angel."

"No problem. I have some other business to handle, but it was great meeting with both of you ladies. I'm looking forward to us having a mutually beneficial working relationship. If either of you have any questions or concerns, please don't hesitate to call me," Angel said as she walked the ladies out.

When Angel got back to her office she noticed she had several missed calls from Laurie, a text that said urgent please call and a voicemail. Angel called Laurie back, but didn't get an answer. "I hope everything is okay with Laurie. I wonder what could be so urgent?" Angel said out loud before checking her voicemail.

"Turn on the local news right now!" Aspen screamed out the moment Taren answered her cell phone.

"Hold on a minute. I was getting something from my car."

"They'll be on to the next story by the time you get to your apartment. Keep your phone close. I'ma call you right back after the news lady finishes talking," Aspen said and quickly hung up.

Taren grabbed the bag she left in the car and then rushed to get back to her apartment. She wanted to catch the news so she could see what the hell Aspen was talking about. By the time she got back to her place and turned on the television Aspen was calling her.

"Girl, what was on the news?" Taren asked sounding out of breath from running up the stairs.

"Have you heard from Laurie yet?" Aspen questioned.

"No!"

"Me neither." After waiting around for an hour or so and calling Laurie numerous times with no answer, Aspen and Taren decided to leave the lounge. They stopped by her apartment, thinking maybe she was upset and bolted on them after seeing the man she said assaulted her, but she wasn't home. Now it was the next afternoon and they still hadn't heard from Laurie.

"Are you gonna fuckin' tell me what you saw on the news or keep me in suspense?" Taren huffed.

"They said they found an unidentified black male dead in his car with a gunshot to the head. And get this, he was found in a parking lot near the lounge we were at last night."

"Aspen, are you serious?" Taren could feel her heart racing.

"Yes! What if it's the man that Laurie saw

you talking to last night?"

"Let's not jump to conclusions," Taren said trying to calm herself down.

"I don't believe in fuckin' coincidences. I'm also betting it was Laurie that put the bullet in his head. You saw how unhinged she became after seeing him."

"Aspen, there's somebody at my door let me call you right back."

"Okay! I'ma try calling Laurie again."

Taren got off the phone with Aspen and walked slowly to answer her door. She was freakin' out over what Aspen had just told her. She picked up her pace when the pounding on the front door got louder. "Coming!" she yelled out.

"I'm glad you're home."

"Laurie! Get in here," Taren said, pulling her inside her apartment before slamming the door. "Where have you been? We've been worried sick about you," Taren said, giving Laurie a hug.

"I'm glad you were so concerned," Laurie said calmly.

"Of course we were concerned. You left last night without saying a word and we haven't heard from you since. Come sit down." Taren took Laurie's hand and led her to the couch.

"Sorry about that, but I had to take care of something."

"Something like what?" Taren swallowed hard, praying that Aspen's suspicions were incorrect.

"I couldn't let him get away with it. That monster didn't deserve to live after what he did to me."

Taren's heart dropped. The worst was being confirmed and she wasn't ready for it. Never did she believe Laurie was built to pull the trigger and take another person's life, but after what she endured everyone had their snapping point.

"What are you saying, Laurie?"

"I waited and I followed him to his car. Luckily, he was alone and I was able to confront him. Do you know he didn't even recognize me at first? This scum who almost beat me to death had the audacity not to remember me. He actually thought that I was trying to come on to him. The nerve. It wasn't until I pulled out that gun, did he take me seriously." Laurie's eyes watered up, but it wasn't due to sadness but for the rage she still had while telling her story.

"Laurie, I'm so sorry. I wish you'd brought Aspen and me with you. You shouldn't have gone through that alone." Taren's voice sounded full of compassion.

"You sound so sincere."

"That's because I am." Taren seemed puzzled. "Is there something wrong, Laurie?"

"Is there... you tell me."

"Laurie, you've been through a lot and I'm sure whatever went down with you and Tony last night made things even worse."

"How did you know his name was Tony? I thought you said you didn't know him."

"I don't know him. I remember the name he gave me when he introduced himself last night," Taren replied, trying to quickly cover her tracks.

"I see." Laurie nodded.

"So what did happen?"

"What do you think happened?"

"I'm not sure, but I was on the phone with Aspen right before you came over. She told me that a man was shot and killed last night near the lounge we were at."

"I see."

"I have to ask, Laurie. Was it you? Are you the one that killed the man?" Laurie didn't respond. She sat on the couch, locking eyes with Taren. But it seemed she wasn't looking at Taren, but through her. "Can I get you something to drink or eat?" Taren offered, wanting Laurie to open up, but she continued to sit quiet. "I'll be right back."

On her way to the kitchen, Taren thought about calling Aspen, but opted against it. She decided it was best if she talked to Laurie on her own first and got all the information she could before calling Aspen back. Taren poured them both a glass of water and grabbed some Pringles before heading back to the living room.

"Laurie, what are you doing!" Taren gasped. She was completely caught off guard and almost dropped the two glasses of water she was holding.

"What does it look like?"

"You're pointing a gun directly at me. You need to put that away. Now!" Taren directed, but Laurie didn't budge. "This isn't funny, Laurie. Put that gun away right now."

"You really are in the wrong profession. Instead of selling pussy you should've went to Hollywood and pursued an acting career. Unfortunately for you, it's too late to use all the fucking and sucking skills you've learned on directors and producers to secure a role in a movie. Why the sudden silence... trying to figure out your next lie, Taren?"

"Laurie, you're not making any sense. Put the gun down so we can talk about what's bothering you. Please," Taren pleaded.

"You know all the right words to say, but none of it means shit to me. I know what you did, Taren!"

"Laurie, what are you talking about? I haven't done..."

"Shut up you conniving bitch!" Laurie hollered. She moved closer to Taren, almost jamming the gun in her face. "Tony had that same fear in his eyes right before I pulled the trigger."

"Laurie, I need you to calm down. You're not behaving rationally and it's scaring me."

"You should be scared because you're about to sustain the same fate as Tony. It's amazing what people will confess to when they're looking down the barrel of a gun, desperate to save their life."

"I don't know what Tony told you, but it's all lies. I don't even know that man."

"Oh, so you don't know the man that you had almost beat me to death. I believe that's highly unlikely."

"That's what he told you? Laurie, he's lying to you," Taren insisted.

"You're good. Even with your back against the wall, the lies keep flowing effortlessly. But give it up, Taren, I know everything. Tony told me how you all plotted together and how badly you wanted to bring Angel down starting with her business."

"Laurie, I can explain."

"Explain what? How you devised a plan to have a man you were fuckin' beat me to the brink of death, just to make Angel's business fail. You wanted the girls to stop working for Angel because they felt their lives were in jeopardy and you used me as the sacrificial lamb to make it happen. Then what, you start your own escort service and planned on taking all of Angel's girls and clients with you. You are truly a piece of work, Taren."

"When I saw you lying in that hospital bed, it made me sick to my stomach. Tony wasn't supposed to hurt you like that... I swear."

"So instead of giving me two black eyes he was supposed to give me one. Or instead of him fracturing both my arm and leg he should've chose one or the other. Is that what you mean?"

"I made a mistake, Laurie. A huge mistake and I'm so so sorry."

"You're a liar! Angel has been nothing but good to you and all this time you've been plotting behind her back. With all that scheming it still didn't get you what you wanted. You're not half the woman that Angel is. She needs to know that the person she considered her best friend was actually her worst enemy."

"I understand you're upset and you have every right to be, but we can fix this. I can make things right, Laurie. This can stay between the two of us. No need to get anyone else involved."

"You don't get it, do you?" Laurie let out a sinister laugh. "You're more disgusting than the sonofabitch who assaulted me. You pretended to be my friend and you were the one who set all this in motion. You ruined me. I can't even walk down the street without looking over my shoulder. I live in constant fear not trusting anyone especially a man. My life has forever changed because of your selfish, greedy ass. I'm doing the world a favor by erasing you from it," Laurie stated with venom dripping from every word.

Taren knew she needed to act fast. The sweet Laurie that wouldn't hurt a fly no longer existed. The new Laurie wanted blood and she had no problem pulling the trigger to get it.

"Well, lookie here," Laurie taunted, glancing at her cell phone. "I think I should answer this... it's Angel calling."

Laurie was distracted for a second as she decided whether or not to take Angel's call. Taren knew this would probably be her best and only opportunity to make a move. Not putting any more thought into it, Taren threw the two glasses of water she was holding in Laurie's face. Being fast on her feet, she then reached down to retrieve the heavy vase on the coffee table, slammimg it as hard as she could over Laurie's head multiple times. Laurie's limp body fell to the floor as blood gushed from her head.

"Look what you made me do, Laurie!" Taren screamed out loud as she processed the magnitude of what she had just done. She shook her head back and forth, pacing the floor not sure what her next move should be.

Fuck! Why did you have to go after Tony, Laurie? You should've left well enough alone. Eventually you would've gotten over what happened and moved on with your life. But no, you had to play vigilante and seek revenge. Now look at you, on my living room floor in a puddle of your own blood. You leave me no choice, now I have to kill you, Taren thought to herself.

Chapter Thirteen

Gone Girl

"Babe, you've been on your phone all morning. Is everything okay?" Darien questioned Angel before kissing her on the neck.

"No. I've been trying to get in contact with Laurie for a couple days and I keep coming up empty. It's really strange."

"Stop worrying. That girl probably went away for a few days with some guy she dating or something. Does she have a man?"

"No, she doesn't. But she called me several times a couple of days ago, sent me a text, and left a voicemail. It's not like Laurie to vanish like this. I've been sending text messages out all morning to the girls to see if any of them have heard from her."

"Have they?" Darien asked as he got dressed for his morning workout.

"Not one of them has seen or heard from Laurie in the last few days. If I were in Miami, I would be getting in my car right now and driving to her apartment to find out what the hell is going on."

"Is that your way of telling me you're ready to go home?"

"I'm actually enjoying Vegas, but I can't lie, I'm super worried about Laurie. She hasn't been the same since that night she was assaulted, but she seemed to be getting better... back to her old self again."

"Angel, seriously, stop worrying. I'm positive that girl is fine. You don't need to be stressin' over this," Darien insisted. "This another reason I wish you would walk away from your escort business. You way too wrapped up in these girls' lives."

"I'm not tryna hear nothing you saying when it comes to Angel's Girls. That's my company and I have no intentions giving it up anytime soon so enjoy your run." Angel shot Darien a fake wave and smile and exited the bedroom.

"Aspen, will you please put that cigarette out? I've seen you smoke more in the last hour then the entire time I've known you."

"I need something to calm my nerves. Not only is my purse still missing so is Laurie. I'm giving her until tomorrow. If I don't hear from Laurie, I'm going to the police station to file a missing persons report."

"Are you sure that's a good idea? You wanted to go to the police about Angel too when she was MIA for a few days, but aren't you glad you didn't. She popped back up on the scene a couple days later."

"This is different, Taren. Angel didn't disappear from a lounge and take my purse with her, a purse that had a loaded gun inside. Let's not forget Laurie saw the man that assaulted her too, who could be the very same man found with a bullet to the head. Laurie could be somewhere hurt or gotten herself in serious trouble. We need to find out and our best option is the police because I don't know where she could be."

Taren heard the words coming out of Aspen's mouth, but she wasn't listening to them. She was too busy thinking how Aspen was standing in the exact location Laurie was, when she pointed a gun in her face. She then thought about how the light went out in Laurie's eyes after getting pounded over the head with a heavy vase. Taren's mind then jumped to the moment she decided to kill Laurie, by placing a pillow over her face and shooting two bullets in her head to guarantee she was dead. Finally, she squeezed Laurie's petite body in a large suitcase and rolled it down to her car before placing the dead body in the trunk. Taren remembered waiting for it to get dark, before driving an hour or so outside of Miami, to a remote lake, where she dumped Laurie's body, then headed back home.

"Taren, do you hear me?" Aspen barked. "You need to snap out of whatever world you're in and come back to reality."

"I was listening. I heard everything you said. Can we talk about something else though?

I'm tired of discussing Laurie. She's our topic of conversation every damn day," Taren complained.

"Let me get out of here." Aspen sighed. "I have work in a few hours so I need to go home and get ready."

"Aspen, I apologize for spazzing out about Laurie. I guess I'm scared because I'm worried something bad happened to her too."

"No need to apologize. I know how much you care about Laurie, we all do. The fact that no one can get in touch with her has us all on edge. Maybe you're right and Laurie will pop back up in a few days like Angel did."

"Yeah, I'm sure she will," Taren said, knowing damn well Laurie's dead body was floating in the water somewhere.

"I'll call you later." Aspen gave Taren a quick hug before leaving.

Taren headed straight to the kitchen and poured herself a glass of wine. She sat down on the barstool, twirling around in her seat. Taren was trying to drink away the guilt of murdering Laurie, but in her mind she had no choice. Her guilt soon turned to bliss. Laurie and Tony, the only people that knew her involvement in everything were dead and her secrets died with them or so Taren thought.

Taren got up to pour herself another glass of wine when her cell began to ring. She picked up her phone and saw it was Angel calling. "Hey, Angel! How are you?" Taren put on an extra chipper voice as if all was perfect in her life.

"I'm doing okay."

"Only okay? You should be doing great. You have the perfect boyfriend, successful business... everything that a girl could dream of."

"I guess you're right," Angel said, feeling a tad awkward not from what Taren said, but how she said it. "But I wasn't calling to talk about my life. I was calling about Laurie."

"Yeah, we still haven't heard from her," Taren said taking a sip of wine straight from the bottle. She was searching for a quick rush to calm her nerves.

"The last day Laurie was seen or heard from, she called me several times and sent me a text saying to call her and that it was urgent."

"Did you call her back to see what was so urgent?" At this point Taren was becoming so stressed, she was close to finishing the entire bottle of wine in one gulp.

"I did, but I was never able to get her on the phone."

"I'm sure it was nothing serious." A sense of

relief came over Taren knowing Angel never had an opportunity to speak to Laurie directly.

"Maybe or maybe not. She left me a voicemail." Taren wasn't expecting Angel to spill that tea and almost spit out her wine when she did.

"A voicemail… what did she say?"

"That she had something very important to talk to me about regarding you. What was that noise?"

"Oh, nothing. I'm standing outside so that could be anything," Taren lied, looking down at the kitchen floor. There were broken pieces of glass from the wine bottle she just dropped when Angel told her about the voicemail Laurie left.

"Okay. So ummm about the voicemail Laurie left me. Do you have any idea what she wanted to talk to me about regarding you?"

"I don't have a clue."

"Are you sure, Taren? Laurie wouldn't just call me and say that for no reason." Angel wasn't letting up and Taren knew she was no dummy. If she wanted Angel to back off, Taren had to come up with a better answer.

"You're right. We thought it was better not to tell you because we didn't want you to worry."

"Who is we and what didn't you want me to worry about? Answer me Taren," Angel pressed.

"Me and Aspen. The three of us went out a few nights ago and Laurie saw me talking to this guy."

"And...."

"She said the guy I was talking to was the man that assaulted her."

"What! Who was the man and how do you know him?"

"I didn't know him. He was trying to talk to me when I went to the restroom. I had no idea who he was. I explained that to Laurie, but she was freaking out. Maybe she didn't believe me, I don't know."

"Why didn't you or Aspen tell me this from the jump?"

"Because Laurie disappeared that night and she took Aspen's purse with her. Aspen had been carrying a gun ever since Laurie was attacked and had it with her that night."

"So Laurie has Aspen's gun?"

"Yes, but there's more." Taren paused.

"Well, spit it out!" Angel snapped.

"A man was found dead in his car right near the lounge we went to that night and we haven't heard from Laurie since."

"You all think Laurie killed that man?"

"We're not positive and we didn't want to

say anything until after we spoke to Laurie but..." Taren's voice trailed off.

"I wish you all would've told me this instead of keeping it from me." Taren could hear the frustration, anger, and concern in Angel's voice.

"You're right, we should've said something, but we were trying to protect Laurie. Neither one of us wanted to believe she was capable of murder even if it was the man that assaulted her."

"Anyone is capable of murder if put in a certain predicament," Angel said thinking about the time she murdered a man to protect Gavin.

"True, but you never know. Laurie could show up at any moment and tell us she had nothing to do with that man's death."

"Yeah, but with every day that passes, it becomes more and more unlikely. Thanks for finally telling me the truth, Taren."

"Of course. Again, I apologize for waiting so long. I thought Laurie would've showed up by now. But since she hasn't, you deserved to know what was going on."

"Thanks, Taren. I'll talk to you soon."

When Angel got off the phone with Taren she immediately made a beeline to her man.

"Darien, I need you to do something very important for me."

"Anything, babe. What is it?"

"I need you to find out everything you can about a man that was murdered a few nights ago outside a lounge in Miami."

"I'll get one of my men on it. Is there any information in particular you're looking for?"

"Not sure, but I have a feeling whatever you do find out, will make things a whole lot clearer for me."

Angel stood in front of the massive window looking out at the Vegas Strip. She wasn't sure why, but something about Taren's story and Laurie's disappearance didn't feel right to her. Taren could very well be innocent in all of this, but Angel's gut instinct was screaming something entirely different and she planned on getting to the truth one way or the other.

Chapter Fourteen

Valley Of Death

"Boss, I have some bad news," Elijah came into Nico's office and said.

"I haven't been back in Miami for a full twenty-four hours and you have bad news already? What the hell happened now?"

"We finally located Tony."

"Where the fuck is he?"

"The morgue."

"What! The bullshit don't stop. How in the fuck did he end up there... besides being dead of course." Nico exhaled, tossing his pen down on his desk.

"He was found with a bullet in his skull outside a lounge. It was on the news, but it took a minute for him to be identified because his wallet wasn't on him. It was actually the car that was registered to one of our businesses that had them reach out to us. I went down and identified his body."

"Damn. I hate that that happened to Tony. Do the police have any idea who killed him?"

"Not yet, but they're going over some surveillance footage that might've caught the murder on camera."

"Keep me posted on that. Still nothing on Angel?"

"Not yet, but I have some leads I'm working on that I'm almost positive will pan out." Nico appreciated the confidence in Elijah's voice, but he wasn't willing to give it too much weight until he presented some receipts.

"I'm counting on that. If you're not able to locate Angel, I might need to reassess your position within the organization, because you might not be the man for the job," Nico stated.

"I need to get back to handling some business and I know there is no shortage of work you need to deal with, so you can go now," Nico said dismissively not even bothering to look up before Elijah left.

Elijah walked out of Nico's office more determined than ever to locate Angel. He desperately craved Nico's approval and acceptance. He admired and borderline worshipped his boss. He wanted Nico to think of him as indispensable and Elijah was willing to do anything to make that happen.

"Nathan, just the man I wanted to see," Elijah called out when he noticed Nathan about to leave. "I'm glad I caught you before you left."

"Is everything a'ight?" Nathan asked closing the door.

"No. As you can imagine, Nico is pissed off."

"Hell, I am too. I can't believe someone murdered Tony. We gon' find the motherfucker that did it too," Nathan seethed.

"Nico isn't pissed about Tony."

"Then what?" Nathan's face frowned up.

"That we haven't located Angel."

"Angel... that lil' bratty ass bitch that someone did us a favor by taking off our hands. We lose one of our men who risked his life on a daily basis protecting Nico and he concerned about a teenybopper. What is Nico's fascination with that girl?" Nathan questioned, getting amped.

"I know you and Tony were close, but you need to watch your mouth. Nico is our boss and I won't stand here and let you disrespect him," Elijah warned.

"What you need for me to do?" Elijah could still hear a bad attitude in Nathan's voice, but he knew Nathan was a loyal worker and would fall in line.

"For one, lose that attitude. Then, I need you to stop by this address," Elijah said, handing Nathan a piece of paper.

"When I get there then what?"

"Park somewhere discretely and monitor everyone going in and out of this gym."

"That's it?" Nathan inquired.

"For now. But make sure you pay close attention. I'll call you in a few hours for an update."

"I'll head there now and wait for your call," Nathan said and left.

"May I speak to Angel Riviera?" The unfamiliar voice on the other end of the phone caused Angel to waver for a moment.

"Who's calling?"

"This is Detective Morrison of the Miami PD."

"This is Angel, how can I help you?"

"I'm investigating the murder of Laurie Hamilton. Can you tell me what your relationship was with her?" There was dead silence on the phone. "Miss Riviera, are you there?" the detective called out.

"Yes, I'm here. I apologize, but I'm having a hard time digesting what you said."

"I understand so I'm assuming you had a personal relationship with Miss Hamilton."

"She actually used to work for me and we were also friends."

"What kind of work?"

"I run a modeling agency and she was one of my models."

"I see. According to her phone records you were the last person she called and sent a text message to."

"Are you serious? Laurie has been dead since then?"

"There hasn't been any phone activity on this number since that call so it's a strong possibility."

"I didn't get a chance to speak with Laurie that day. When I called her back I didn't get an answer."

"Her text message said urgent. Do you have any idea what was so urgent?"

"No idea," Angel lied. She had no intentions of telling the detective about the voicemail Laurie left her. "Can you tell me how she died?"

"She was shot and thrown in a lake. Fortunately, her body was washed up, or she might've never been found. Do you have any idea who would want Laurie dead?"

"Nobody. Everyone loved Laurie."

"Interesting. Since Laurie has been dead for over a week, is there a reason you didn't file a missing person report?"

"She was working through some personal issues so Laurie hadn't worked in the last few months. I was very concerned when I didn't hear from her, but I was hoping she just needed some time to herself and would reach out to me when she was ready."

"What kind of personal issues?"

Angel debated if she should tell the detective about the assault. She wanted Laurie's killer to be caught, but Angel didn't want to steer the investigation in her direction. If that happened, it could easily place unwanted attention on her escort service.

"She never said. When I tried talking to her about it, I couldn't get her to open up."

"Thank you for your time, Miss Riviera. Please take my number. If you think of anything that might help with the investigation give me a call."

"I will," Angel said, writing down the detective's number.

Angel hung up the phone on the verge of tears. She remembered the first day meeting the bubbly blond and how she was the initial inspiration to start Angel's Girls. Laurie loved having fun, partying, and having sex with rich good-looking men. Angel knew there were a lot of women who were just like Laurie, but instead of them having casual sex for free, she turned what they did for fun into a money making machine. Now Laurie was dead and it broke Angel's heart.

Chapter Fifteen

Lies Intertwined

"I can't believe Laurie is dead," Aspen sobbed.

"Me neither," Beth cried, wrapping her arms around Aspen.

Angel had arranged for all the ladies that worked for Angel's Girls to come together and mourn Laurie's death in a suite at the Four Season's Hotel. The room was decorated with white and pink roses, Laurie's favorite colors. It was catered with everyone's favorite foods and drinks. Angel wanted the ladies to be comfortable even though they were gathering under the saddest of circumstances.

"Everything looks so beautiful. Laurie would've loved this," Cherie said between sniffles.

"Yeah, she would've. Angel had them do an amazing job," Dawn added.

"Too bad Angel couldn't be here," Taren said to the other girls as they sipped on champagne.

"Taren, can I speak with you for a second," Aspen said, taking her hand.

"I was coming, you didn't have to grab my hand, Aspen."

"You could've given me a heads up that you told Angel what happened that night at the lounge," Aspen snapped. "I was completely taken off guard when she called me about it."

"Sorry, I forgot. It wasn't my intention to tell Angel, but I didn't have a choice. I meant to tell you, but we've both been busy lately and it slipped my mind. What did you tell her?"

"The truth. She didn't think it was a good idea that I was running around with an unregistered gun, but other than that she said if I ever kept the truth from her again, I would be out of a job."

"Don't stress, she'll get over it."

"Maybe, but unlike you, I'm not Angel's childhood best friend so I don't get the same passes as you."

"I hear you, but I'm not on the best of terms with Angel either.

"If only we could go back to that night. I would do so many things differently and maybe Laurie would still be alive."

"Aspen, what happened to Laurie has nothing to do with us. We didn't leave her, she left us," Taren barked.

"Instead of leaving her at the table, one of us should've stayed with her or maybe the three of us should've left right then. What I do know is Laurie was in no condition to be left alone."

"Tomorrow is Laurie's funeral. I think we need to focus on that instead of the what if's we can't do anything about." Taren was trying to sound like the voice of reason so Aspen could stop dwelling on that night. The sooner everyone forgot about Laurie, Taren thought, the better off she would be.

"Detective Morrison, I think you need to see this," Officer Harrison came over to his desk and said.

Morrison put his finger up letting Harrison know to give him a second, as he wrapped up a phone call. Once Morrison was done he went over to an interrogation room where Harrison and another officer were watching a video.

"Is this what you wanted me to see?" Morrison questioned, nodding his head at the television where the video was playing.

"Yes, take a look. Make sure you watch closely."

Harrison sat on the edge of the table, watching carefully not wanting to miss a thing. The footage was a little blurry, but you could clearly see a man being shot execution style. At first Harrison wasn't that intrigued until he got a glance of the shooter.

Morrison couldn't believe what was unfolding right in front of his eyes. Never did he imagine that one murder investigation would be linked to another. "That's our victim, Laurie Hamilton... and she's our perp."

"I don't think it's a good idea for you to go to Miami," Darien said as Angel was packing her clothes.

"I have to go. Not only was Laurie a friend, but also it's important that I be there for the other girls. Right now we need unity."

"Then let me come with you."

"You need to train for your upcoming fight. I won't be gone long, I'm coming right back. You're already having two of your bodyguards go with me. I'll be fine, baby." Angel smiled, giving Darien a kiss.

"I don't like you being out of my sight. After almost losing you, I can't take any chances."

"You're not going to lose me. We've taken all the necessary precautions," Angel reassured him.

"I never told you this, but the night you went missing, I planned on proposing to you."

"Are you serious?" Angel dropped the blouse she was about to put in her suitcase and stared at Darien.

"Very. With everything going on, I could

never find the right moment to give it another try," Darien said as he started to get down on bended knee.

"What are you doing?" Angel put her hand over her mouth, stunned by what she was seeing.

"I figured I need to stop trying to find the moment and just make it happen. Angel, would you do me the honor of being my wife?"

When Darien opened the small velvet box, Angel wasn't sure what astounded her more, Darien's proposal or the gigantic rock that he was about to put on her finger. Angel's eyes watered as disbelief kept her from speaking.

"Baby, say something," Darien said nervously. "Are we going to make this official or what?"

"Yes! Yes! Yes!" Angel jumped up and down and screamed.

"This ring looks perfect on you. Exactly the way I pictured it." Darien kissed Angel's hand. "You're my queen and I can't wait to spend the rest of my life with you."

"I feel the same way, baby." Darien and Angel held each other not letting go as if to stop time, so that the moment would never end and last forever.

Chapter Sixteen

Secrets Will Catch Up To You

"Babe," I'm about to go," Angel called out while walking down the stairs. When she got to the bottom, from a distance she could see Darien at the front door walking someone out.

Angel glanced down at her watch and noticed she had more than enough time to stop by her office to retrieve something. Before she even had a chance to sit down, Darien came in.

"Hey! Did you hear me call out to you?" Angel asked, turning on her computer.

"Yeah, I did. I was walking someone out and he was talking so I got distracted. When I looked up you were gone. I figured you were in here dealing with work."

"You know me. If my mind isn't on you then it's on business," Angel beamed.

"At least I come first."

"Always. So who came to see you this early?"

"The man I had dig up some information on the dude that was killed."

That was all Darien needed to say to get Angel off the computer and direct her full attention to him. "Did he find out anything?"

"Sure did. His name is Tony Palmer."

"Damn, why does that name sound so familiar?" Angel questioned out loud although she was actually asking herself.

"Here is the information the man gave me. He also included a picture," Darien informed Angel, handing her the manila envelope.

"Wow, he even included a photo," Angel commented before puling it out.

"He's thorough, that's for sure."

"Oh my fucking goodness!" Angel gasped.

"What's wrong?"

"I know this man."

"How?" Darien was surprised that Angel would even know a man like Tony, since according to his source he had an extensive criminal record.

"He worked for Nico. He was one of the men that kidnapped me."

"Word! Well, that's probably why his name sounded familiar to you."

"No, that's not where I heard his name, but I do remember his face because I remember thinking to myself that he looked Jamaican. So this is the animal who assaulted Laurie," Angel shook her head in disgust.

"You're sure he was one of Nico's men?"

"Positive... but hold on a sec. I think I know why that name sounds so familiar." Angel kept meticulous records, which was about to prove beneficial. She pulled up an excel file that had all the names of previous and current clients in alphabetical order. "I knew it. That sonofabitch was a client."

"Of yours?" Darien was shocked and so was Angel.

"Yes. He was a steady client for a few months and then he suddenly stopped. He would always request Taren."

"Yo, that's crazy. So the guy that worked for Nico, used to be one of your clients?"

"Exactly and Taren said she didn't know him, but that's obviously a lie. The reason I never tied him to the assault on Laurie was because he used a different name. Slick fuck," Angel seethed.

"So why did Taren lie about knowing him?"

"Evidently because she has something to hide and I'm going to find out what that is."

Taren dreaded getting out of bed the morning of Laurie's funeral. Putting on all black and listening to people mourn was not how she wanted to spend her Saturday afternoon. The only thing that made it tolerable was knowing this time tomorrow it would all be over. Taren had no interest dedicating any more of her precious time on the woman she killed.

"Oh gosh who could this be?" The knocking on the door was not a distraction Taren welcomed. She wanted to drink her orange juice in peace and be left alone, but that wasn't in the plans. "Good morning. I wasn't expecting to see you until later on at the funeral," Taren said, letting Aspen in.

"I know, but I started getting in my feelings again. I thought maybe we could go together," Aspen suggested.

"Sure, we can do that."

"Thanks, Taren. I was hoping you said that. I even brought what I'm wearing so I can get dressed here. I know I've been a downer lately, but I appreciate you being here for me. I'm taking Laurie's death a lot harder then I thought I would."

"It's understandable. People handle death differently."

"You've been handling Laurie's death well and I admire you for it. I'm still having nightmares. I can't remember the last time I slept all night."

"Maybe you should take some sleeping pills. At least until the sadness settles down."

"Is that how you're dealing with things? Unlike me you look relaxed and well rested."

"I have been sleeping like a newborn baby. I'm sure it's due to the sleeping pills," Taren lied and said. She wasn't missing out on a minute of sleep over Laurie. In fact, the reason Taren was sleeping better than ever was because she felt all her lose ends had been neatly tied up. It didn't stop her though from plotting on Angel. Taren blamed her for her father's death and destroying her life in the process.

"Then you need to pass a few of those sleeping pills over to me. I'm tired of not getting my eight hours of sleep."

"No worries. I got you. Remind me to give you some after the funeral."

"I will." Aspen let out a long sigh then plopped down on the couch taking off her shoes. "Have you heard from Angel? Is she coming to Laurie's funeral?"

"I haven't spoken to her so I don't know, but probably not. I think she's still trying to stay low key."

"That's too bad. I miss having Angel around. I know she's our boss, but she seems more like a girlfriend. Maybe because she's our age." Aspen laughed.

"Yeah, I guess... but umm I'm about to get in the shower and get ready for the funeral. You can use the other bathroom."

"I was getting so comfortable on your couch, but let me get up." When Aspen stood up she let out a high-pitched scream. "Ouch!"

"What's wrong?"

"I stepped on something," Aspen moaned,

looking at the bottom of her foot. "Oh goodness. I'm sorry, Taren."

"Sorry for what?"

"I stepped on your emerald earring. It's so pretty too, but I think I broke the back."

"Let me see," Taren said, quickly grabbing the earring from Aspen's hand.

"I hope they weren't too expensive."

"Don't worry about it," Taren said throwing up her hand. "It shouldn't take me that long to get ready."

Taren hurried to her bedroom, closed the door, and locked it. *Fuck! I thought I cleaned everything up. How could I have been so stupid and missed this earring. When I hit Laurie over the head with the vase, it must've somehow flown off her ear. Aspen didn't seem suspicious so I think I played it off good. I have to be more careful. I can't afford to make dumb mistakes like that because I don't wanna have to kill Aspen too*, Taren thought to herself before getting in the shower.

When Detective Morrison arrived at the church,

Laurie's funeral had ended. Friends and families were leaving the building, but he recognized the person he wanted to speak to from a photo he found online. He then made a beeline in her direction.

"Angel, I'm so glad you were able to come." Aspen gave her a warm hug.

"It is good to see you. I was surprised when you walked in," Taren added also giving Angel a hug.

"There was a delay with my flight. I'm just happy I didn't miss the entire service."

"Miss Riviera, I hate to interrupt, but I need to have a few words with you."

Angel, Taren, and Aspen were all caught off guard when the lanky man in a basic blue suit walked up on them, interrupting their conversation.

"How do you know me and what can I do for you?"

"My apologies, I'm Detective Morrison," he said flashing his badge. "I spoke to you on the phone recently."

"Yes, I remember. I thought I answered all of your questions."

"You did, but there have been some new developments in the case and I wanted to ask you a few more questions."

"Then ask. Aspen and Taren were also friends of Laurie so I'm sure they would like to hear what those new developments are too."

"We were able to go over some surveillance footage from the night before Laurie was murdered."

"And?" Angel wanted the officer to get to the point.

"Do you know a Tony Palmer... any of you?"

"No." The three ladies said in unison.

"Mr. Palmer was also murdered recently and Laurie Hamilton was his killer."

"Really? I can't imagine Laurie killing anyone. Was he trying to rob her or hurt her in some way? The only way I could see Laurie killing someone was in self defense," Angel stated while Taren and Aspen nodded in agreement.

"No, it wasn't self defense. Miss Hamilton shot and killed an unarmed man. Or maybe there's more to the story and one of you can assist me with that."

The three women all stood with blank stares on their faces. They had no intentions of assisting Detective Morrison with anything and he knew it.

"I'm sorry that I couldn't be of any help."

Morrison's beady blue eyes were telling Angel everything she needed to know. She was on his radar and if she wasn't willing to give him the information he needed then Angel should watch her back.

"I won't take up any more of your time, Miss Riviera, but I'll be in touch."

"I'm sure you will. Enjoy the rest of your day, Detective Morrison."

Chapter Seventeen

Give Me The Reasons

"I was pleasantly surprised when you invited me out for lunch today." Taren gazed across the table, but Angel had her head down, cutting into her tilapia. "I know you've had a bunch of shit going on lately so it's nice that you made time for me."

"I try to make time for my friends. We are friends aren't we, Taren?" Angel continued eating her tilapia waiting to see how Taren would respond.

"What type of question is that?"

"The type of question I want you to answer." Angel put down her knife and fork, finally locking eyes with Taren.

"Of course we're friends. We've known each other practically our entire lives. You're like the sister I never had."

"That's what I thought too."

"What changed? I realize you were upset that I didn't come to you about Laurie and you had every right to be. But I don't think it warrants you questioning our friendship."

"Maybe not, but you lying about Tony Palmer does."

"What are you talking about, Angel? Like I told you, I don't know Tony."

"So you want to sit there, look me in my eyes with a straight face, and tell a bold face lie. Is that the bullshit you on, Taren."

Taren swallowed hard not sure how to respond to what Angel said. There was no doubt she knew something, but Taren wasn't sure how much and that made her vulnerable. She treaded lightly feeding off whatever Angel said next.

"I'm not bullshitting, Angel. I want to make

things right between us."

"Then I'll ask you again. Do you or don't you know Tony Palmer?"

"Yes, I do," Taren admitted, only because she had no choice. She had known Angel long enough to be able to read her body language. It was obvious to Taren that Angel had made the connection between her and Tony. To continue to deny it would only do more harm than good.

"How well do you know him?"

"He used to be a regular customer of mine."

"So why did you lie to me about that? Why did you pretend you didn't know who he was? And I want the truth. No more lies, Taren."

"I started seeing him off the books."

"Meaning behind my back so you can keep all the money?" Taren nodded her head yes. "I see. I always thought I was extremely fair money-wise with my girls."

"You are."

"Then why take the chance of ruining not only our business relationship but our friend-ship."

"I had no choice."

"You always have a choice, Taren."

"It was my mom. Angel, she hit really hard times. She developed a real bad drug habit and my Aunt kicked her out. I was desperate to take care of her because she had nothing."

"Why didn't you come to me, Taren? I would've helped you."

"I was too embarrassed. Growing up I would always brag that my mother didn't have to worry about getting a job or working because of her looks a man would always take care of her. When you would say that you wanted to make your own money so you could take care of yourself, I would laugh at you," Taren looked down as if ashamed. "But you were right. After my father died she was never able to recover. My mother had no skills, she started letting herself go and began dating a guy that got her hooked on drugs."

"I had no idea, Taren."

"How would you? I didn't want you or anybody else to know how hard she had fallen. When Tony suggested we keep seeing each other without him going through you and he would pay me more, I took him up on the offer. But he began getting really possessive and aggressive. I started putting him on ice, ignoring his calls. That's what we were arguing about when I saw him at that lounge."

"You're talking about the night Laurie saw you with him?"

"Yes. He had threatened that if I didn't start seeing him again he would tell you about the arrangement we had. I was freakin' out. Then when Laurie said he was the man that assaulted her, I was terrified. I didn't know what to do so I just pretended that I had no idea who he was."

"Taren, I wish you would've come to me." Angel put down her napkin and stared off as if in deep thought.

"I do too. I let the shame I felt about my mother cause me to make some really bad choices. I have so many regrets and then poor Laurie. Tony had become very aggressive with me, but never did I think he was the sort of monster that would do what he did to Laurie."

"Tony was also one of the men that kidnapped me," Angel revealed to Taren, but she already knew, since she played a pivotal role in making that happen.

"Are you serious! Tony kidnapped you, but why? Do you think it had something to do with what happened to Laurie?"

"No, it's totally separate, but for some strange reason it all feels connected, but how, I don't know."

"Tony Palmer is an animal. It might be an unfortunate coincidence that he came to our lives," Taren reasoned.

"That's true. But I don't know...." Angel's voice faded off as if back in deep thought.

"Trust me, I'm not trying to make a habit of this, but can you forgive me for not being upfront with you? I really value our friendship and I don't want to keep doing things to jeopardize it."

"Of course I forgive you. We're like family, but Taren you have to trust that you can come to me. You don't have to be embarrassed about your mom or anything else. I'm your best friend and I'll never judge you, that's not what friends do."

"Thank you, Angel." Taren stood up from her chair and walked over to hug Angel. "I don't know what I would do without you."

"You don't have to worry about that. We're going to be best friends forever," Angel said, hugging Taren back.

"Speaking of forever, I'm sure you know I noticed that ridiculously beautiful ring on your finger."

"Oh, that little thing." Angel and Taren both laughed.

"Does that mean you and Darien are engaged?" Taren asked.

"Yes, he proposed before I left and of course I accepted."

"You really do have it all, Angel. I'm truly happy for you."

"Thank you! Of course you'll have to be my maid of honor."

"I wouldn't have it any other way." Taren was smiling on the outside, but her jealously boiled over on the inside. The happier her so-called best friend appeared the more determined Taren was to bring Angel down for good.

Darien was finishing up his core exercises with his trainer as he prepared for his upcoming fight. It was imperative for boxers to build up their core muscles to protect against body punishing shots and Darien made sure he was in top-notch condition. He was using a heavy medicine ball as his back was against the wall. His knees were bent at 90 degrees and he was in the sitting position, but not actually sitting on anything. After fifteen minutes, his abdominals were on fire, but he wouldn't let up. Darien was holding the medicine ball straight out in front of him and then lifting it above his head then returning it back in front. It was just a part of Darien's grueling workout, but a crucial one and one of the reasons he was the undisputed welterweight champion of the world.

"As always you put in that work today," Darien's trainer said as he began his cool down.

"I ain't trying to give up this championship belt. Gotta put that work in," Darien scoffed.

"You got this!" his trainer kept saying, keeping Darien hyped. He was ready to go another round.

"I ain't done yet!" Darien barked when he noticed Keaton come in. He continued with his cool down, annoyed that Keaton had disrupted his focus, but Darien kept going until his trainer told him he was done.

"Good workout." The trainer patted Darien on the shoulder.

"Thanks," Darien said, using his towel to wipe the sweat off his face.

"Sorry for interrupting your workout, but I got a phone call I thought you would want to hear about immediately," Keaton informed Darien.

"What sort of phone call?"

"He's waiting in the living room to tell you himself."

"Why the fuck is you talking in riddles. Tell me what the fuck the phone call was about and who is waiting for me," Darien demanded to know.

"Steph Nunn. He wouldn't give me the details. He said you had him look into some things and he got that information you wanted regarding Nico Carter. When he couldn't get you on the phone he called me. I told him you were training, but to come over so he could speak with you when you were done."

"See, wasn't that easy."

"I wasn't sure if you wanted me to say all that in front of your trainer. I know he's been working with you for years, but I also know how private you are about certain shit," Keaton explained.

"No doubt. Let's go see what Steph talkin' 'bout."

"Mr. Blaze, I understand you were in the middle of training, but I thought you would want to hear what I have to say."

"I'm done and I do. Talk to me, Steph."

Steph looked over at Keaton as if reluctant about speaking in front of him.

"You can say what you know in front of Keaton. He's a trusted worker and friend," Darien informed Steph.

"Apparently Nico Carter has a disgruntled employee within his organization because he was willing to give me some interesting information for a price."

"Have you paid it?"

"I did. Of course I'll add it to your bill."

"Well spill it and it better be worth the price 'cause I'm sure it wasn't cheap."

"I know why Nico Carter has taken such an interest in your girlfriend..."

"That would be fiancé," Darien corrected Steph.

"My apologies. Your fiancé."

"Why?"

"She's his daughter."

"What the fuck are you talkin' about. No way. That's not possible."

"Yes, it is. I demanded proof before I would pay. He produced a copy of the paternity test that Mr. Carter had done recently," Steph said, handing the paper over to Darien. "As you can see it was done recently."

Darien dissected every inch of the paper. He saw the date the test was done and it was during the time Nico was holding Angel hostage. Darien balled up the paper and threw it down.

"How many people know about this?" Darien questioned.

"I don't think many. My source says that

he found the test locked away in Nico's office. He believes that Mr. Carter is trying to keep the information very low key. His behavior while Angel was staying there..."

"You mean held against her will!" Darien roared.

"Yes, that's what I meant... while Angel was being held against her will, Nico's attitude towards her raised suspicion within his organization. Originally, his plan was to use her to get to you. But without notice to anyone else, Nico changed those plans. He kept Angel away from everyone. Only the lady that runs his home was allowed to see her. He was very protective."

"I get it... I get it!" Darien growled not wanting to hear about how the man he detested was some protective father to the woman he planned on spending the rest of his life with. "You can go now," Darien said, dismissing Steph. "You can send me your final bill."

Keaton walked Steph out and came back to see Darien still fuming. He was standing by the window as if he was about to put his fist through it.

"Nico Carter isn't one of your favorite people, but maybe he'll be a better father-in-law," Keaton joked.

"That shit ain't funny."

"Sorry, I just hate seeing you upset like this. It might not be that bad. Maybe once Angel knows that Nico is her father, you all can squash this beef."

"Fuck that! Nico doesn't deserve to have Angel in his life and she doesn't need to know that the man who kidnapped her is her father."

"What are you saying... you're not going to tell Angel that Nico is her father?"

"That's exactly what I'm saying. This shit stays between us."

"Man, I don't know about this. You can only keep Angel hidden away for so long. Eventually Nico will find her and tell her the truth."

"Not if I can help it."

Darien Blaze was so used to winning rounds in the boxing ring that he assumed that it would naturally transcend to every day life. But he had never dealt with an opponent like Nico Carter. Keeping father and daughter apart may prove to be the one fight that he would lose.

Chapter Eighteen

Nothing Will Ever Be The Same

Elijah sat at the bar watching from a short distance as Amber and Baily were having dinner with two local businessmen, Gabe and Dalton. The men were partners at a high-end car dealership in Vegas. The girls had come in wanting to buy a pair of matching white Mercedes Benz. They said they made money together so they wanted to ride in style together... their words. The problem was the women had nothing to show as proof of income but cash. But those were the exact type of clients that Gabe and Dalton welcomed.

Elijah had been doing business with the men for years. They were the typical upper level drug dealers that tried to launder their profits in a legitimate business venture. So when Elijah got word that Darien had an upcoming fight he followed a hunch and decided to take a trip to Vegas and do some asking around. As if divine intervention was on his side, Elijah happened to be at the car dealership when Baily and Amber showed up and showed out.

The ladies bragged that they were working for a modeling agency called Angel's Girls and although they didn't have any pay stubs they had more than enough money to put a hefty down payment on the rides. This was the sort of break Elijah had been waiting for and he took full advantage. Gabe and Dalton owed him plenty of favors and Elijah was cashing in on one right now.

"This is the first time I've ever been to Prime and the food is delicious," Amber commented as she nibbled on her truffle mash and seafood platter. "I've always heard about the Bellagio fountain show, but to be able to eat a delicious meal and have a window view of it... doesn't get much better than this."

"Sure doesn't," Baily chimed in glancing around at the striking chocolate brown and delicate Tiffany blue décor. There were prominent pieces of artwork on display. As well as a water-themed canvas screen and a garden patio with the perfect outdoor setting for a tranquil dining experience.

"I was thinking after dinner we could go back to my house and have some more drinks by the pool," Gabe proposed.

Amber and Baily looked at each other as if having a silent conversation with their eyes.

"Sure, that sounds great." The ladies smiled. They all took a few more bites of food, finished off the champagne, and the four of them headed out with Elijah discreetly following close behind.

Amber and Baily thought that they had met their potential husbands when they arrived to Gabe's home. It was the perfect blend of contemporary elegance and state-of-the-art automation.

"Who knew selling cars had you living like this," Baily whispered to Amber.

"You ain't lying," Amber replied, unable to stop oohing and awing over the layout of the home.

When you entered through the interior courtyard, a cascading waterfall combined with fire and distinguished architecture welcomed you to an understated, remarkable residence. Soaring ceilings highlighted the custom wall of marble in the formal living room and it showcased beautiful fairway views that surrounded the home. Clean lines, neutral tones, and a sophisticated design created an aesthetically soothing environment that flowed from room to room effortlessly. There were finishes such as elegant fabric walls in the dining room, travertine flooring throughout, limestone accents, and warm rope lighting were just a few features that set the breathtaking ambiance.

Gabe gave the women a full tour of his unbelievably beautiful home and they savored every moment. The gourmet kitchen was sleek in design with top-of-the-line appliances and a tasteful contrast of dark custom cabinetry and light, slab countertops. The luxury estate included an automated home cinema, fitness center, game room, home office, wine cellar, four bedroom suites, and an amazing attached casita. The master suite, situated on the main level, resembled something out of a luxury magazine quality. It had a spa inspired master bathroom that made you not want to leave the house.

"Let's go out to the backyard and open this bottle of champagne," Dalton said, as the ladies wanted to stay in the master bedroom and crawl into the massive king sized bed.

The backyard of the home was equally as extraordinary as the inside. It was perched high above the fairway; sweeping views could be enjoyed in every direction, including multiple fire pits, a full outdoor kitchen with a built-in television, and a serene infinity edge pool.

"Have a seat," Gabe told Amber and Baily as he handed everyone a glass and poured the champagne. As the ladies got comfortable with the outdoor living space, Elijah felt it was the right time to make his presence known.

"We have company." Baily grinned, welcoming the young yet distinguished looking man.

"This is our friend Elijah. He'll be joining us," Dalton said.

"Great, the more the merrier." Amber giggled.

"Hello, ladies. This should be a very interesting evening." Elijah folded his hands and sat down next to the women.

"Baby, I'm so happy you're home." Darien held Angel tightly as their wet lips locked and they kissed for what seemed like eternity.

"Wow! I need to go away more often. This has to be one of the best kisses ever."

"There's more of where that came from," Darien continued sprinkling kisses on Angel's neck.

"Say no more." Angel smiled, leading Darien to the bedroom. The two lovers undressed each other with such passion and intensity. Every time Darien would slide inside of Angel it felt like the first time to him and to her it felt like she never wanted to be touched by another man again.

After they made love, Darien put his arm around Angel's warm naked body and pulled her close. He moved her hair away from her ear and whispered, "I want us to get married."

"I thought that was the point of you giving me this gorgeous engagement ring," Angel said admiring the huge diamond decorating her finger.

"I don't want to wait. I want us to get married before my fight."

Angel lifted her body up and stared at Darien as if she misunderstood what he said. "Did I hear you correctly? You want to get married before your fight?"

"Yes. I don't wanna wait."

"Why the rush? I thought you wanted to have a beautiful lavish wedding?"

"I do and we can, but that's going to take a lot of planning. I'm ready for you to be Mrs. Darien Blaze. I want us to have a small ceremony as soon as possible and then plan the most extravagant wedding for our friends and family."

"You know my mother and grandmother are both dead. I don't know who my father is so I don't have anyone to walk me down the aisle. You're my only family and Taren who is like a sister. Of course I'll invite some of the girls who work for me, but it will mainly be your friends and family there."

"Baby, I'm everything you need," Darien said, kissing Angel.

"You're right. Having you in my life makes up for all the loses."

"Does that mean we can go ahead and have that small wedding ceremony before the fight and then go all out later on?"

"Yes, my love," Angel leaned in and gave Darien a kiss.

"You're about to make me the luckiest man in the world."

"Ditto to you, babe."

"Elijah, you haven't had one glass of champagne. All you've been drinking is bottled water. Don't be a party pooper." Baily laughed.

"Not at all. The party is just about to get started."

"Is that right! Does that mean you boys want to turn things up a bit. Maybe take a dip in the pool... naked!" Amber suggested and Baily joined in.

"Not that sort of party ladies," Elijah said calmly. Amber and Baily both had a slight buzz, but they were far from drunk and they could tell the vibe was off.

"I'm not following you," Baily was the first to speak up.

"Then let me explain it to you." Elijah's once friendly voice had now taken on a serious, intimidating tone. "You ladies are going to do something for me. We can go about it the easy way or you can make it much more complicated."

"Listen, we're not models we're escorts. If you want sex all you have to do is pay for it. We're not into anything rough so please don't do anything crazy," Amber pleaded. The women were both nervous and regretted ever hooking up with the men. They feared they were dealing with some quacks who wanted to rape and torture them.

"I don't want to hurt you," Elijah reassured them. I just need your assistance on a rather important matter. If you do what I ask, those pretty white matching Mercedes Benz you ladies want... I'll buy them for you."

Amber and Baily's fear had now turned to complete confusion. They didn't understand what the hell was going on, but Elijah did have their undivided attention.

"What do you want from us that's worth you buying us cars?" Baily asked almost afraid to hear the answer to her question.

"The two of you work for Angel's Girls."

"Yeah." they nodded.

"I need to meet with your boss, Angel Riviera."

"I can give you the number. You can call and make an appointment." Amber shrugged. "Is that it?" she questioned with a raised eyebrow.

"What do you think?" Elijah stood up and said. He didn't believe the girls were Ivy League scholars, but he also didn't think they were that dumb either.

"Will you please tell us what you want?" Baily shouted.

"Calm down. I'll tell you, but just so you know, this isn't a request. You either do it or suffer the consequences."

"Are you threatening us?" Amber asked nervously.

"Yes, I am." Elijah said it so matter-of-factly that it sent a chill down Amber and Baily's spine. "Now that you understand this is a do or die situation, let me explain exactly what you ladies are going to do for me."

Chapter Nineteen

Make You Proud

Nico sat in his office and something seemed off to him. He looked around his desk and nothing appeared out of place, but at the same time something felt different. It was neat... a little too neat. He buzzed for Margaret.

"Margaret, can you come to my office for a moment."

"Of course, Mr. Carter."

Nico tapped his fingers on the desk not able to shake off the uneasy feeling.

"What can I do for you, Mr. Carter?"

"Margaret, have you been in my office and straightened up at all in the last couple days?"

"No, sir." She shook her head. "I know you don't like for anyone to come into your office when you're not here, including me."

"True. Have you noticed anyone else come in here when I wasn't home?"

"No, sir, I haven't. Is there something missing?"

"No, not missing, just," Nico's voice trailed off. "No worries. You can go now."

Nico kept his office door locked when he wasn't home. But there was a spare key in case an emergency came up and he needed one of his workers to get inside. No such emergency had come up in the last few days so none of them would have any reason to use it. Nico had an inkling that someone had used the spare key, the question was who and why. He knew where to start for answers.

"Hey boss," Elijah answered.

"You still out of town handling business?"

"Yes, sir."

"How's it coming?"

"Even better than I had anticipated. I believe I should have an update about the whereabouts of Angel for you tomorrow," Elijah stated confidently.

"Really? I hadn't realized you made that much headway." Nico was getting a surge of excitement at the idea of finding his daughter.

"Yes, I'm looking forward to giving you more details soon. Was there something else you were calling about?"

"It can wait. Get back to dealing with the Angel situation. We'll talk tomorrow." Nico hung up the phone and this tremendous sense of happiness came over him. He felt that every day that passed he was losing precious time with his daughter. The sooner they connected the sooner Nico believed they could start working on building a father and daughter bond.

The excitement of that made Nico forget all about his suspicions regarding someone snooping around his office, at least for the moment. If Elijah came through and brought Angel back to him then he would forever be indebted to him. He would make sure that not only would Elijah have a permanent position in his organization, but that he would receive all the perks that came with it. In Nico's eyes, Elijah would reach the level of being irreplaceable, a status that no one had ever been able to secure with him. Now if only Nico could get that call about Aaliyah, he continued to pray.

Elijah could hear how proud Nico was of him when they were on the phone. He was tempted to tell him that he had actually found Angel and tonight she would be with him, but Elijah held back. He wanted to wait until his plan unfolded impeccably and then revel in his Nico's praises. Elijah was so adamant about keeping his plan close to the chest to avoid unwanted problems that besides calling in a favor from Gabe and Dalton, he only brought in Nathan to assist him with securing Angel. Nathan had proven to be loyal and able to follow directions without fucking up. When Elijah had Nathan go monitor the comings and goings at a gym, it proved to be beneficial. Darien Blaze's personal trainer owned the gym.

After a couple of hours of watching the traffic coming through, Nathan informed him it wasn't much. Elijah then had Nathan go inside asking to speak with the owner because he wanted to hire him as a personal trainer. The overly talkative receptionist informed Nathan that she would take down his information, but the owner was out of town training Darien Blaze for an upcoming fight. But she promised he would give him a call once he was back in town. Not only did Nathan come through with the useful information, but he also honored Elijah's request to keep what he found out between the two of them.

Once Elijah was able to confirm Darien had an upcoming fight, if he wasn't training at the Miami gym like he typically did, then Elijah reasoned he might be in Vegas, since that was where the upcoming fight was taking place. His hunch had paid off. Now here Elijah was, getting dressed in preparation of getting Angel back for Nico.

While Elijah was securing his weapons, he heard a knock at the door. "Right on time," he said looking down at his watch. "Glad you made it." Elijah opened the hotel room door to let Nathan in.

"You already know, when you call, I'm here," Nathan said, taking a seat. "I'm still waiting for you to tell me why I'm here."

"How was your flight?" Elijah questioned as if purposely dodging Nathan's question.

"It was cool. Typical flight. So how long are we staying in Vegas? You told me to get a one-way flight. Does that mean we're chillin' here for a minute?" Nathan was prying for info, but Elijah was holding on to it tightly.

"Nathan, I had you come here because I believe you're the most competent and loyal out of all Nico's men, excluding myself of course."

"Of course." Nathan nodded with a smile. "But seriously, I appreciate you saying that about me though, man."

"You're going to like what I'm about to say even better. If we... not if, but when, we get this job done, both of us will be in a much better position in Nico's organization. That means more responsibility which equates to more money."

"I like the sound of that."

"I knew you would."

"So what do we have to do?" Nathan was becoming anxious waiting for the answer.

"We're here to get Angel and take her home to Nico."

"She's here... you found her?"

"Yes. Shortly, she's going to be meeting two women at the restaurant here in this hotel for dinner. When the time is right we'll snatch Angel up and take her back to Miami on the private jet."

"So that's why you had me get a one-way flight, we going back on the jet. Works for me. I'm assuming the two women Angel is having dinner with are working with you."

"They actually work for Angel, but on this particular matter, yes they're working with me," Elijah explained.

"I know I'ma do my part, but are you sure you can put your faith in those women to do theirs?"

"I have faith that they don't want to die so they'll do precisely what I ask."

"Being able to stay alive is good motivation," Nathan cracked. "But on a serious note, since we know where Angel is, why do we need those two women?"

"Because Darien has bodyguards on her at all times. Angel and Darien are actually staying here at the hotel, but again security is extra tight. I needed those women in order to get Angel somewhat alone. I wouldn't be surprised if Darien has security escort her to dinner, but between the two of us we'll be able to handle them, mainly because we got them beat due to the element of surprise. I had them try to talk

Angel into meeting at an outside restaurant, but she wouldn't agree. That might essentially end up working in our favor."

"Why is that?"

"Because if Angel left the hotel, it's a guarantee that Darien would have her escorted with security. With her having dinner at the hotel, at this point they've been staying here for a while so I'm sure they've gained a certain level of comfort. Maybe that comfort will turn into them being a little lax."

"That makes a lot of sense."

"I agree. We can continue our conversation on the way to the elevator," Elijah said, looking at the time. "We need to go... it's showtime."

Chapter Twenty

Chess Moves

"We're getting married in one week."

When those words came out of Darien's mouth, Angel damn near fell over and broke the heel on her electric blue Giuseppe Zanotti suede strappy sandals, while zipping up the back.

"Baby, be careful." Darien caught Angel's hand before she completely lost her balance.

"You can't drop something like that on a girl

when she's zipping up five inch heels." Angel shook her head. "Babe, I get that you wanted to get married soon, but a week? I can't plan a wedding, not even a really small one in a week."

"You don't have to. I'm making all the arrangements. I want our wedding day to be even better than what you imagined and it will be."

"Oh really? I'm not sure if I should be grateful that I don't have to go crazy trying to put everything together or upset that you're not including me with the planning," Angel huffed.

"Don't have a tantrum. There's no reason for you to be upset. It was my idea for us to get married right away and I want to show you how appreciative I am. I know you would rather wait and have your dream wedding and we will. But I also want to make this wedding a dream so it's only right I handle the preparations. It wouldn't be fair to put that stress on you."

"That's sweet of you to take my feelings into consideration."

"Always. I'm going to plan the best one week notice wedding ever... you'll see." Darien chuckled.

"Coming from you, I don't doubt it," Angel said, zipping up her floral print high-waisted pleated shorts with side pockets.

"You look beautiful," Darien commented as Angel tightened the strap on the floral print crop bustier that matched her pleated shorts. "I'm tempted not to let you walk out the door."

"No worries, I'm not going far. I'm meeting Baily and Amber at the restaurant downstairs in for dinner."

"Save room for dessert with me."

"Dessert? I thought you cut out all sweets while training?" Angel asked, shocked that Darien would break his workout diet regimen.

"I'm about to do another workout session with my trainer, so I think a bowl of fruit with some whip cream won't do too much damage."

"You call fruit and whip cream dessert? Boy, stop!" Angel burst out laughing. "Tell you what, you have some fruit and I'll have some cake. We can share the whip cream and call it even."

"Deal!"

"Okay, babe, I'll see you when I get back." Angel gave Darien a kiss and headed out.

"Hold up! Where you think you're going?"

"I just told you, silly."

"Wait while I call for a couple of guards to escort you down."

"Darien don't! I'm going to the freakin' hotel restaurant. I'm not leaving the building. I don't want two men all in my face while having dinner with two women that work for me."

"Angel, it's for your own good. I don't want anything to happen to you. Like before."

"That's not going to happen. I love how protective you are of me, but I don't want to feel like a prisoner 24/7. So please let me have one evening security free. That was the main reason I had the girls meet me here instead of going out so I wouldn't need bodyguards."

"Okay, baby. You win. But be careful and if anything seems off to you, call me."

"I will, but I'll be fine. Love you." Angel blew Darien a kiss then winked her eye.

"Love you, too." He grinned, catching the kiss.

"Can you lay off the fuckin' drinks!" Baily snapped at Amber, while they sat at their table waiting for Angel to come down.

"I don't know how you can be so calm. These drinks are the only thing that's making it possible for me to sit at this table and pretend nothing is wrong." Amber reached for her wine glass, but this time Baily snatched it away.

"Listen, I'm not trying to die tonight. If we just do what the fuck he said, we can all walk out of this hotel alive."

"How do we know this Elijah dude isn't lying to us? He could very well take Angel and kill her, then kill us too."

"Amber, he doesn't want to hurt her."

"So he says!" Amber shot back looking wild eyed. "Angel has been nothing but good to us. If something bad happens to her because of this, I'll never forgive myself."

"Omigoodness, stop. Your eyes are getting all watery. Here!" Baily shoved a napkin in Amber's hand. "Wipe your face before Angel gets here," she said sternly.

Amber dabbed her eyes to keep the tears from trickling down her face. She then reached in her purse and took out a small mirror to fix her makeup. "I pray this all works out. Gosh, we should've kept our mouths shut. If we hadn't went in the car dealership, boasting and bragging, they would've never known we even knew Angel." Amber shook her head in despair.

"I don't feel good about this either, Amber. I like Angel… I really do. But I really don't believe that Elijah guy plans on harming her in any way. We just have to stick to the script and Angel will never know the role we played in this and we'll all be okay... sit up and pull it together," Baily mumbled, discreetly hitting the side of Amber's leg. "Here comes Angel," she whispered.

"Hey ladies!" Angel beamed, giving them both air kisses.

"Angel, hi!" the women said in unison.

"You look great as always," Baily smiled. And wow, your engagement ring is even more beautiful than the first time I saw it," she cooed.

"Thank you. I'm still getting used to the "I'm an engaged woman" thing, but I kinda love it." Angel blushed.

"You should because you wear it well. I know you must have a thousand things going on, especially with the upcoming wedding. I know you said the first one will be very small and intimate, but I appreciate you making the time to have dinner with us." Baily was doing her best to keep the mood upbeat since Amber wasn't much help and she didn't want to blow it.

"Of course. Honestly, I was happy you asked. All my girlfriends are in Miami and although I adore Darien, it's nice to hang out with the girls sometimes, especially with two of my best workers. You all have received nothing but positive feedback from all your clients. You are totally raking in the cash."

"Thanks, Angel. A lot of it has to do with you. You're so hands on with us and you give the best advice on how to deal with these men. I really appreciate the pointers." Amber's voice was full of sincerity.

"When you work for Angel's Girls, I want it to be beneficial for both of us. If you win, I win and vice versa. I'm also very impressed with Chandler, Monique, and Allison. They were excellent referrals. Soon, there will be just as many girls working in Vegas as in Miami." Angel was pleased with how her Vegas business was beginning to boom. She felt that bringing Amber and Baily into the fold had a lot to do with it. Not only were they great, but they also brought three new girls in the mix that was awesome too.

"That's always a good thing when the boss is pleased. So I'm glad to hear it, Angel," Baily gushed.

"I am very pleased, but enough about that. Let's get to why you all wanted to meet for dinner."

"I know you haven't known me and Amber for that long, but in this short span of time I feel that we're like family."

"That's funny you say that because I was telling Darien the other day that the women who work for Angel's Girls are like family to me."

"I'm glad you said that because Amber and I were hoping you would let us throw you a bachelorette party. Before you say no... nothing over the top."

"No, Baily, I think that's a great idea!"

"You do?"

"Yes, and thank you for thinking of it. God willing, I'll only be getting married once in my life and every soon-to-be-bride needs a bachelorette party." Angel clapped her hands with enthusiasm.

"Awesome!" Baily shouted as she smacked the side of Amber's leg again, letting her know to perk up. "Isn't that awesome, Amber?"

Amber gave a half ass yeah that Baily wasted no time in covering up. "Let's order a bottle of champagne to celebrate. It's on me." Baily waved over the waitress and put that order in.

"Are you okay, Amber? You don't seem your normal bubbly self," Angel commented.

"Amber didn't get any sleep last night. The people who live next to us were up all night making so much noise. I took sleeping pills so I could get my eight hours of sleep, but poor Amber didn't."

"Yeah, those rowdy neighbors of ours." Amber nodded.

"That's terrible. People can be so rude. Hopefully, you'll be able to catch up on your sleep. You all have a busy upcoming weekend so I want you rested."

"Oh, here's the champagne." Baily cut her eyes at Amber letting her know to get her shit together.

After the waitress filled each of the ladies glasses with champagne Baily had them make a toast. "To your upcoming wedding. May Angel and Darien live happily ever after!" The ladies tapped each other's glasses before taking a sip.

"So you know, Darien told me right before I came down that we're getting married in a week. So you ladies are going to have to move fast if you want to have this bachelorette party."

"No problem. We got you covered, Angel. Amber, show Angel the different venues we were thinking about having her party at."

"Sure." Amber reluctantly pulled out a folder from her purse that contained several different venue options. Baily had gone over the script with her several times, but Amber was finding it difficult to stick to it. Amber scooted her chair closer to Angel. "Let's take a look," Amber said before then pretending to accidentally drop the folder letting all the papers fall out. "I'm so clumsy," Amber said as if embarrassed.

"Girl, please! I put the C in clumsy." Angel giggled, helping Amber pick up the papers. While Angel was distracted, Baily used the opportunity to spike Angel's drink with the drug Elijah gave her. He said the effects wouldn't take long to kick in, so right after Angel finished her drink to get her to the designated area where he would be waiting. Baily used her finger to help dissolve the drug, but the bubbles in the champagne helped to camouflage it anyway.

"I think that's everything," Amber said loudly, to let Baily know they were coming back up. "So sorry about that, Angel."

"Don't worry. Now let me take a look at these venues," she said, going through each piece of paper. "Ummm, this is nice. I love the layout, very sexy."

"That's one of my favorite spots too," Amber agreed. She kept staring at Angel's hand, praying she wouldn't reach for her glass. She became so paranoid; Amber began to wonder if Angel could hear how fast her heart was beating.

"Oh wow, this one is pretty dope too," Angel continued as she started getting excited with all the choices. As Angel placed down the paper and was about to look at the next one, she leaned over and reached over for her glass.

"Don't drink it!" Amber blurted out.

Baily's stare was so intense it almost seemed like she was throwing knives at Amber. "Amber, why are you being so silly." Baily was making a last ditch effort to save face, but Angel was no dummy. Her hand yanked away from that glass like it was on fire.

"I can't do this." Amber put her head down.

"I guess that means we're all going to die tonight," Baily said, biting down on her lip.

Angel had no idea what the fuck was going on, but her motto was always play it cool when shit looked like it was about to go to shambles.

"I need for you to answer one question. Are we being watched?" Angel asked knowing that based on the behavior of the women; they were being used as puppets for someone.

"Yes," both ladies said.

"Okay. I need you all to pull your shit together and stop looking like the world is coming to an end... even if it might be. That means get back to smiling and acting like we're planning a party. Do it now." Angel demanded as firmly as possible without drawing attention to herself.

Both women began smiling and Amber picked up her glass of champagne hoping to get some liquor courage.

"Who put you up to this?" Angel wanted to know.

"His name is Elijah, at least that's the name he gave us," Baily revealed.

"Yeah, that's his fuckin' name. He works for Nico Carter," Angel said while sending a text to Darien at the same time. "I just sent Darien a text, letting him know we're in danger. I should've listened to him when he insisted I have the guards come down with me." She exhaled deeply.

"Angel, I'm so so sorry. Please forgive me. I never wanted to be a part of this. I swear," Amber insisted with tears in her eyes.

"Amber, cut it out. This is not the time to break down in tears. I need you to focus and get some self-control. We can deal with the other shit later," Angel huffed, trying not to get frustrated. "Obviously they wanted you to drug me, then what was suppose to be your next move?"

"He said you were supposed to start feeling a little dizzy soon after finishing your drink. He then said we should offer to take you back to your suite and on our way there he would take over," Baily explained.

"Fuck, Darien hasn't responded to my text yet. He's probably working out and doesn't have his phone on him," Angel shook her head, listening to Baily and talking to herself out loud at the same time.

Since Angel knew they were being watched she didn't want to raise any suspicion by getting on her phone. So she decided to keep her phone on the table and call Darien, but put him on speaker. She lowered the volume before the phone started ringing, but he didn't answer. The call went to voicemail. Angel then called Keaton. He didn't answer either so she sent him an emergency text.

"What are we going to do? If he hasn't already, Elijah is going to start getting suspicious. You haven't touched your drink since I spiked it," Baily said becoming anxious.

Trying to think quickly on her feet, Angel came up with a plan to buy a little more time and keep Elijah at bay. She prayed that either Darien or Keaton would get her text so she could get the necessary help they needed.

Angel noticed the waitress was walking towards the table next to them holding a tray of food. Her position would obscure the view between her and Amber. "Amber, slide that empty glass over to me right now! Both of you keep talking and smiling. It has to appear everything is going as planned."

After Amber slid over the glass, Angel discreetly put it between her legs. She then picked up the spiked champagne and pretended to drink it, but poured it into the glass between her legs. Angel then passed the glass back to Amber under the table. While the ladies continued to try and put on a believable show, Angel kept checking her phone, but was getting nothing. She began feeling like the walls were closing in on them. Angel then thought that maybe Nico's men somehow managed to get past Darien's security and had him. She even considered calling the police, but remembered that Darien was adamant he didn't want the police involved with anything that had to do with Nico. He would rather handle it through the streets.

"Elijah just sent me a text saying he saw you drink your champagne and you should start feeling woozy soon, so we should get ready to help you to the elevator shortly," Baily let them know. She had an extra wide smile the entire time telling them so it would look as if they were having random girl talk.

"We're not ready yet, what should we do?"

Amber said panicking.

"Angel, are you listening to us?" Baily questioned, but Angel's mind seemed to be someplace else. "Angel!"

"Chill. I finally heard back from Darien and I was texting him back."

"Thank goodness. What did he say, Angel?" For the first time since she sat down at the table, Amber felt optimistic that they would all be okay.

"He said that security was on their way down and for us to stay at the table until they got here."

"Thank you, Angel. I wasn't sure we were going to make it out of this hotel alive, but now I'm certain we will." Baily smiled. "I really can pour myself a drink now."

"Not so fast," Amber whispered as her bottom lip trembled. "Elijah is walking up on us right now. What do you think he's about to do?"

"We're in a restaurant full of people. He won't do anything stupid," Baily reasoned.

Angel wasn't so sure. She knew they were dealing with a killer which meant none of them could anticipate his next move.

Chapter Twenty-One

Now Or Never

"I'm not feeling well," Angel moaned, putting her hand on the side of her head and lowering it. "Maybe I had too much champagne," she complained, feeling Elijah's presence coming closer. Angel wanted to make sure he heard what she was saying.

"Good evening, ladies." Elijah greeted the women, as he stood directly behind Angel's chair.

"Hello," Amber and Baily replied in a flat tone. Angel kept her eyes halfway closed as if almost completely out of it.

"Your friend doesn't look too good. I thought maybe she might need some help getting out of here. I'll be more than happy to assist." Elijah rested his hands on Angel's shoulders.

Angel tried not to let her body tense up with the touch of Elijah's hands on her. It wasn't easy to pretend she was doped up, but under the circumstances Angel felt this was how she should play it. There was no telling how Elijah would react if he realized she was in on what he thought was a well-orchestrated game plan.

"We were about to take her upstairs. She's staying here at the hotel," Amber said looking over at Baily.

"Yeah, thanks for the help but we got this," Baily added.

"No, she's coming with me," Elijah made clear when he jammed the silencer on his gun in Angel's back. "The plans have changed. The two of you were taking a little too long for my taste."

As Elijah began pulling Angel out of her chair, there was a commotion that could be heard coming from the direction of the elevators. "Come on!" Elijah shouted, yanking Angel's arm.

"Let her go!" Amber yelled.

"Shut the fuck up!" Elijah yelled back, raising his arm to fire a shot at Amber. Angel tried to knock the gun out of Elijah's hand, but he managed to pull the trigger, firing the gun in Amber's direction. At first they thought the bullet missed her until Amber began holding the side of her stomach. "Don't do that again," Elijah warned Angel, as he managed to get her in a headlock.

"I'm bleeding," Amber spoke so softly they didn't hear what she said. It wasn't until she held up her hand and it was full of blood that they knew she had been shot.

"You bastard! You shot her!" Baily hollered, reaching over to help Amber.

"Both of you are useless to me." Elijah then let off another shot, this time hitting Baily. Her body hit the table hard, causing some of the glasses to shatter to the floor. It seemed no one in the restaurant was paying attention to what was going on at their table until what sounded like a crash put everyone on notice. Seeing Amber bent over with blood dripping from her side and Baily's wounded body spread over the table put the entire restaurant in terror mode. People began screaming, jumping out of their seats headed for the exit. The chaos made it easier for

Elijah to try and drag Angel out, but because she wasn't actually drugged, she fought against him every step of the way.

"Damn, you a lil' fighter. If Nico didn't want you alive, I would put a bullet in your head right now," Elijah barked. As he looked for Nathan's whereabouts, he noticed there were a couple of injured bodies by the elevator and three other men were all shooting in the same direction. *Fuck! I bet those are Darien's men and they're shooting at Nathan,* Elijah thought to himself. *I fucked up. I should've brought in more manpower. I can't think about that shit right now. I have to get the hell out of this hotel.*

Angel peeped the frustration on Elijah's face while he watched Darien's men in a gun battle with who she assumed was some of Nico's men, although she couldn't see them. While Elijah was distracted he had loosened his grip on Angel's neck so she made her move. She clamped her teeth into his arm as hard as she could, drawing blood. Elijah struggled to get his arm out of Angel's mouth, but she didn't stop there. She had more freedom to move so Angel jammed her heel into his groin area.

Elijah's bellowing like a wounded animal caught the attention of Darien's men. Two of the men continued shooting and the other darted towards Elijah firing shots in his direction. While Elijah returned fire, Angel made a run for it. She ran back to the restaurant to check on Amber and Baily. Neither the police nor the paramedics had shown up yet so Angel called 911. Amber and Baily appeared lifeless, but Angel was praying for a miracle that both women could be saved.

"You made it!" Nathan said when he saw Elijah open the hotel room door.

"Barely," Elijah grumbled. Sitting down on the edge of the bed looking at the bite mark Angel left on his arm. "I can't believe that bitch bit me," he shook his head.

"Man, we almost get killed to get that broad and you don't even have her! Like what the fuck!" Nathan growled, flinging his arm.

"My fault. I didn't count on Darien sending an army of his men down to attack. I fucked up, all because I wanted to impress Nico. I don't know how I'm gonna explain this shit to him. For whatever reason he was hell bent on getting

Angel back alive and I wanted to be the one to make that happen. Now he'll look at me as a major fuck up," Elijah sulked.

"I like you, Elijah, I really do. But this need you have to please Nico, a nigga that don't give a fuck about anybody but himself is a major problem."

"What are you talkin' about, Nathan?"

"You wanna know why Nico is so fuckin' pressed about that Angel broad... because she's his daughter."

"Huh?" Elijah looked dumbfounded.

"You heard me. She's his daughter. I did some snooping in Nico's office and found the paternity test he had done."

"You went into Nico's office? Are you fuckin' crazy! You know what's gonna happen to you when he finds out."

"I don't have to worry about it, 'cause he ain't gon' find out," Nathan barked.

"Yes, he is because I have to tell him."

"Of course yo' bitch ass do. You probably wish you could bend over and get fucked by that nigga. But you don't get it. Nico don't care about you. You see how he dismissed Tony's death like it was nothing. You ain't nothing to him neither... none of us are. You only matter to Nico Carter if you got his DNA running through your blood," Nathan spit.

"Nathan, fuck you! I thought you were a loyal soldier, but I was wrong about you. You not a team player. Get the fuck out my room. If I was you, I wouldn't report back to work because trust me when I tell you, you're fired."

"Nah, nigga, I quit and if you would get your head outta Nico's ass, you would realize you're playing on the wrong team. You could've been on mine but it's your loss." Nathan chuckled before putting two bullets in Elijah's head.

Chapter Twenty-Two

Friends Make The Best Enemies

When Amber opened her eyes, the first person she saw was Angel sitting on a chair. She appeared to be sleeping, but when Amber called out her name Angel instantly looked up.

"Hey there! I was about to doze off. How are you?" Angel asked.

"I'm okay. Happy to be alive," Amber gave a slight smile. "I've always hated hospitals," she said glancing around her room.

"I know how you feel. I don't talk about this much, but my mom died in a hospital after giving birth to me. So yeah, I have a love/hate relationship with hospitals."

"I'm so sorry to hear about your mom. I doubt you ever get over something like that."

"No, you don't, but you learn to live with it."

"Angel, I know I said it before, but I'll say it again. I'm so so sorry for what we did to you. I honestly felt like we didn't have a choice, but that's still no excuse," Amber sobbed.

"Don't cry, Amber." Angel got up from her chair and sat down on the bed next to Amber. "This isn't your fault. Nico, Elijah, and his men are responsible. You tried to do the right thing before it was too late and probably saved my life in the process."

"Thank you for being so forgiving. Baily didn't want to be a part of it either. I hope you'll also forgive her. How is she doing?"

"I wanted to wait and tell you this but..." Angel turned away before continuing. "Baily didn't make it. She died at the restaurant. I'm sorry, Amber."

Angel held Amber closely as she cried her heart out. Amber loved Baily and knowing she would never see her friend again left her feeling broken. Angel knew that feeling all too well and promised herself that she would be there for Amber as much as she needed her.

"Nathan, where have you been?" Nico questioned when Nathan showed up for work after going missing for the last couple of days.

"Boss, I was in Vegas with Elijah."

"Vegas? Elijah had you in Vegas with him?"

"Yes. He had me come to help him with something very important he was working on for you. Elijah told me not to say anything and that he would deal directly with you about me being away once we got back."

"I see. So where is Elijah now? I tried calling him a few times today and I haven't been able to reach him."

"Boss, things didn't go as planned. We were this close to bringing Angel to you, but Darien and his men ambushed us. Unfortunately, Elijah is dead and Darien killed him."

"Damn! Elijah sounded so confident on the phone when I spoke to him. He should've told me what he was up to so I could've brought in some help."

"I agree. I had no idea what he was up to until I got to Vegas. He was being very secretive with everything. He said I was the only one he trusted to help him get Angel, but I feel like I let him down."

"Elijah put you both in a bad position. The two of you should've never been going up against Darien and his men alone. Now Elijah is dead and Darien's punk ass is the one responsible. It's time I got rid of Darien Blaze for good," Nico said, pacing his office. He thought about how Darien was keeping him from his daughter and now had killed one of his best men. Nico knew that if he didn't annihilate Darien soon, he might destroy any chance he had of reuniting with Angel and that would happen over his dead body.

Taren was on her way to her Brazilian wax appointment in preparation for meeting with a couple of clients later on that evening. She had taken a few days off for no good reason, but now her pockets were empty and Taren was ready to put in that work. She had her window down, letting that Miami breeze blow through her hair and had her music blasting. It was so loud that she missed the first call from Angel. But when a song came on the radio that Taren didn't like, she turned down the volume and that's when she heard her phone ringing the second time.

"Hey Angel," Taren said, sounding extra happy to hear from her, although the sound of her voice made her cringe.

"What you doing girl?"

"On my way to get a wax before I work tonight."

"I know that's right. Nothing like a well groomed girl." Angel laughed.

"Yeah, well the business we're in everything has to be on point. Competition is stiff out here."

"You ain't lying. But the customers love you so you straight," Angel assured her. "But I didn't call you to talk about work."

"So what's up?"

"I've had so much drama going on recently."

"Like what?" Taren wanted to know.

"Girl, there is too much to tell on a phone call especially for one that I can't stay on long. When we hook up for dinner and drinks I'll tell you all about it."

"Can't wait!" Taren said frowning at her phone.

"But anywho, Darien decided to move up the wedding. We're having a small ceremony next week."

"What, are you serious... why?"

"He doesn't want to wait. Darien is ready for me to be Mrs. Blaze and honestly with all the bullshit I've endured lately so am I. We're going to have an elaborate wedding in a few months, but we're having a very intimate wedding in Hawaii first. So I'm going to still need your Maid Of Honor services in the near future." Angel giggled.

"Girl, you know I'm game. I can't wait, but your Hawaiian wedding sounds very romantic. Give me all the details," Taren smiled as she took notes on everything Angel said.

Chapter Twenty-Three

Made Myself A Boss

"I can't believe we're really getting married today," Angel beamed in the mirror.

"Believe it. Tomorrow this time you'll be Mrs. Darien Blaze... my wife. I like the way that sounds."

"I love the way that sounds, too." Angel stood up and twirled around in her floor length ivory silk bathrobe.

"Not more than me." Darien reached out and pulled open Angel's robe, revealing her lace bra and panties.

"Don't even try it!" she said, slapping his hand away. "We are not having sex right now."

"Come on, baby." Darien started kissing Angel on her neck.

"Forget it!" Angel moved away from Darien with a flirty smile spread across her face.

"You know you want to."

"Of course I do," Angel agreed. "After we get married today, I want tonight to be like our first time."

"Every time I make love to you it feels like the first time." Darien said, gazing lovingly into Angel's eyes.

"You always make me feel so special. That's one of the things I love most about you."

"You are the most special person in the world to me and I'm going to spend the rest of my life showing you." Darien placed a sweet kiss on Angel's forehead, wrapped his arms around her waist, and held her tightly.

Aspen was sitting outside by the pool lounging with Beth and Dawn, two other girls that worked at the escort service. The three of them all had a rare day off and decided to chill by the pool in Aspen's condo complex. The Miami sun was shining bright with a calming breeze that made the heat bearable.

Aspen began taking some selfies in her iced kiwi colored, fringed macramé halter with matching cheek fringe bottom. The retro suit had braided ties with bead and tassel detail. The color popped against her deep caramel complexion and she wanted to share with all her Instagram followers. After taking several pictures, Aspen began scrolling through her other pics and came across the photos that she, Taren, and Laurie took before they headed to the lounge and once they first got there. It was the last time Aspen had ever seen her friend alive. Her eyes began watering up seeing how happy they all looked in the pictures.

"Aspen, what's wrong? You look like you're about to cry," Beth said, noticing how misty eyed

Aspen was.

"Is it something you're looking at on your phone?" Dawn asked, noticing Aspen was staring long and hard at her iPhone screen.

"Yeah, it's the pictures we took with Laurie the night before she died. This is my first time looking at them in weeks. I almost forgot I had them."

"Can I see them?" Beth questioned.

"Sure." Aspen handed Beth her phone and she looked at them with Dawn.

"The three of you look like you were having so much fun. And look at Laurie making that goofy face. She loved to clown around." Beth laughed. "I love that green top Laurie is wearing."

"Me too. It matches her emerald earrings. I was with her when she bought those earrings. Her birthday was in May so Laurie got emeralds because of her birthstone and I got ruby since that is my birthstone." Dawn smiled.

"Can I see my phone for a second," Aspen said ready to snatch it out of Beth's hand. Luckily, she handed it over quickly and Aspen zoomed in on the picture.

"Is something wrong, Aspen?" Dawn could see that Aspen's solemn face had changed to a mixture of shock and panic.

"I'm fine. My emotions are getting the best of me thinking about Laurie," Aspen lied. There was something wrong... very wrong. When Dawn mentioned the emerald earrings Laurie was wearing in the picture her mind immediately went into overdrive. Aspen hadn't even noticed or paid attention to the earrings in the photo until now. She couldn't believe they looked exactly like the earring she stepped on at Taren's apartment.

How would one of the earrings Laurie was wearing the night before she died be in Taren's apartment. That would mean Laurie had been there after we went out that night and before she got killed. Taren said she hadn't seen or talked to Laurie since she left us at the lounge, but that has to be a lie. Why would Taren lie about that unless she knows something about Laurie's death or she's the one that killed her, Aspen thought to herself.

Aspen tried to get the possibility of Taren being Laurie's killer out of her mind. She tried to come up with valid reasons why Laurie's earring would be in Taren's possession, but none of the scenarios worked. Aspen couldn't decide if she should confront Taren first, go to the police, or call Angel and let her decide how to proceed. As she wrestled with her options, the only thing

Aspen didn't waver on was that she would get justice for Laurie.

Angel stood in front of the floor length mirror staring at herself. Although she and Darien were having a very small ceremony, Angel couldn't pass on wearing a custom made wedding dress. It was much simpler than the one she planned on walking down the aisle in, as hundreds of guests watched, but it was a beauty nonetheless. The elegant silk mermaid gown with straps, a rhinestone beaded detail at the natural waist, and a crystal covered illusion back fit Angel flawlessly.

Angel couldn't pull herself away from the mirror. She felt like a real life doll. As Angel continued admiring how angelic she appeared in her dress, she was unable to shake the sadness that also loomed over her. It broke Angel's heart that her Grandma Eileen wasn't there to meet her future husband or watch them exchange vows.

Next she shed a tear for her mother. A woman she never had an opportunity to hug or kiss. Angel held the picture she brought of her mom as a single tear trickled down her cheek. But her greatest sadness came from not having her father to share her day with. It was tradition for a father to walk his daughter down the aisle. Angel always dreamed that if she was ever blessed enough to find a man she wanted to spend the rest of her life with that she too would have her father walk her down the aisle. Angel was finding it difficult to accept that wouldn't be her destiny. What did bring Angel solace was knowing she was marrying the man of her dreams and they would live happily ever after.

Nico had been replaying a phone call he received a few days ago over and over again. He wasn't positive the information given to him was accurate, but he wasn't willing to gamble against it either. Leaning on the side of caution, Nico executed his plan and if all went well, Darien Blaze would never be a problem again.

Angel and Darien exchanged vows in a chapel with a phenomenal Hawaiian oceanfront view and Poipu Beach. The breathtaking ceremony space was built with a diamond theme, where the outer wall and roof were made from glass that radiated and sparkled in the sun. As the two lovebirds stood at the altar, the sunlight shined on the couple surrounding them with a romantic glow. The white pews and the white glass aisle gave a picturesque backdrop that one would forever remember.

The crashing waves from the tranquil blue ocean were the ideal spot to exchange ceremonial words. Besides the minister, Keaton was the only other person there to witness the union between Angel and Darien. When the two exchanged rings and said their I do's, it was as if their love intoxicated the air.

"I now pronounce you man and wife," were the last words Angel and Darien heard the minister say before partaking in an everlasting passionate kiss. They didn't even bother waiting for "you may kiss the bride". The couple was now husband and wife. This was the happiest either had ever been in their entire life.

Taren leaned over her apartment balcony, listening to some Drake and smoking her second blunt. She was feeling herself.

After Angel confided in her where she and Darien were having their secret wedding and honeymoon, Taren began plotting on how to use the information to her advantage. It didn't take long for her to decide to place an anonymous call to Nico Carter from a burner cell. She knew he would be skeptical, but she was so detailed with the location and the date that her gut told her he would take the bait. Taren refused to let Angel have her happy-ending even if it meant destroying what should be one of the happiest days of her life.

While Taren gloated in her handy work, she got an unexpected text from Aspen saying she needed to speak to her about Laurie. *What the fuck does she have to talk to me about regarding*

Laurie? The hoe dead and been dead. She's good and buried. I thought once the dirt hit her casket we was done discussing Laurie, Taren thought to herself and tossed her phone down. She didn't even bother replying to Aspen's text because she refused to let her fuck up her high. Instead, Taren turned up her music, lit up another blunt, and continued with her one person celebratory party.

After being chauffeured in the white Rolls Royce to their honeymoon suite, Angel knew she could stay there for the duration of the trip and never leave the 2,500 square feet of luxury. The master bedroom had 360-degree views of the island and after making love all day; you could soak in the oversized terrazzo tub. Waterways winded through the rooms, with mother of pearl accents, candles galore, and direct access to a private beach. But if the newly married couple wanted to stay in they could enjoy lounging on the duvet cushion daybeds, with teak furniture, and rose petals scattered on the terrace overlooking the wraparound pool with floating stepping stones. You could have your personal butler serve your meals on the covered dining pavilion or take a shower outdoors or relax in the copper bathtub. It truly was a little piece of heaven in a Hawaiian paradise.

"Babe, you have to stop spoiling me. If you keep exposing me to all this luxury, nobody will want to be bothered with me but you." Angel laughed.

"Oh you didn't know... that's the plan. This is only the beginning. I plan on making up for all the years you didn't get everything you deserved, starting from childhood."

"You're so silly, Darien," Angel teased, nuzzling his nose with hers.

"I'm serious. I want to give you everything your heart desires and more."

"I have everything... you. You're the most amazing husband ever and we haven't even been married for twenty-four hours."

"You're going to really think that once you see this wedding gift I got you." Darien smiled.

"You got me a wedding gift? You've done enough."

"Damn! I left it with Keaton. Baby, I'll be right back."

"Where are you going?"

"To Keaton's room"

"Keaton's staying here too?"

"Yes, but not in nothing like this." Darien chuckled. "We got the best suite in this joint," he bragged, making a silly face.

"Babe, the present can wait until tomorrow. You don't have to go get it," Angel sighed, kissing her husband. "I don't want you going anywhere."

"Angel, I'll be right back," he promised, returning the kiss. "Plus, the gift is way to precious to let Keaton hold on to it. He might forget it don't belong to him and it come up missing. Then I would have to kill him and you would have to help me hide the body and we might have to go on the run... you know the rest." Angel and Darien both laughed at his fictitious story.

"Darien, you have quite the imagination. Now hurry up! I need you back here in my arms."

"I'm ready to be in something much warmer and a lot wetter than your arms," Darien gave a devilish smirk. "I'll be right back," Darien said and gave Angel another kiss before he left.

Angel stood in the center of their hotel suite and twirled around still wearing her wedding dress. "I can't believe I'm Mrs. Darien Blaze," she said, holding up the hand with her wedding ring.

"We did it, baby. We became husband and wife. This really is only the beginning of a wonderful life together. A new chapter that we'll be able to share with our children in the future. Hopefully, on this magical night we'll create our first child together." A glow came over Angel at just the thought of making that happen.

Angel's mind began drifting off thinking of the family that her and Darien would have someday. She imagined a little girl and boy. Then she thought about how her daughter would have the father that she always dreamed of having while growing up and it made her insides fill with joy. As she began visualizing whom their kids would take after, her thoughts were interrupted by a knock at the door.

"Babe, did you forget your key!" Angel said out loud, shaking her head. "Sometimes I think you're more forgetful than me."

Angel opened the door ready to embrace her husband, but instead she was greeted with Darien slumped over on the floor with blood drenching his tuxedo.

"Oh no! Baby, baby what happened!" Angel cried, kneeling down to cradle Darien's injured body. She put his head in her lap and stroked his face. "It's gonna be okay, baby! I promise, it's gonna be okay," Angel kept repeating, rocking back and forth. "Somebody call the ambulance! I need help! Please somebody help me! My husband is dying," she balled as tears flooded her face. "Baby, who did this to you? Who shot you, baby?" Angel stared Darien in his eyes that he could barely keep open.

Darien was trying to speak, but he was so weak and hardly had any strength left. After what felt like an eternity to Angel, he finally mustered up enough force to say, "Nico... Nico Carter," before Darien's eyes closed shut.

Angel was standing in her wedding dress, covered in Darien's blood when Keaton arrived to the hospital. She was holding the jewelry box that was in Darien's hand, when she found him in a pool of his own blood at the door of their hotel suite.

"Angel, what happened?" Keaton questioned. He could see distraught written all over her face, but when she spoke her voice was calm... too calm.

"Nico Carter shot my husband."

"What! When... after he left my hotel room with your gift?"

"Yes."

"Fuck!" Keaton yelled out, punching his fist towards the ceiling. "How do you know it was Nico?"

"Because I asked Darien..." Angel had to pause for a moment before continuing. She swallowed hard, fighting back the tears. She knew Darien wouldn't want her to break down, and instead be strong. "I asked Darien who shot him and he said Nico Carter. That's how I know."

"Damn!" Keaton kept saying over and over, shaking his head.

"I want you to get on the phone right now and call the necessary people because by this time tomorrow I want Nico Carter dead. Do you understand me?"

"Hold on a minute, Angel. I can't even imagine what you're going through right now. But are you sure you want to have Nico taken out? I mean, right now the wounds are fresh and you're making decisions based on emotions. Take a few days... give yourself some time." Keaton didn't want Angel to do something she might regret, especially since he knew the truth and he was tempted to tell her. He didn't believe that Angel would want to be responsible for the death of her own father even under these circumstances. Right when Keaton was about to tell her, he thought about Darien, his boss and childhood friend. Then decided to keep the truth to himself.

"I'm Mrs. Darien Blaze. That means you work for me. I'm your boss. I don't care what it cost. You get on your phone and make this happen... now, because Nico Carter is a dead man!" Angel stated without flinching.

A KING PRODUCTION
MEN OF
The Bitch Series
AND THE WOMEN WHO
Love Them
JOY DEJA KING

Chapter One

Adrenaline Rush

Before Precious Cummings stole their hearts, there was another woman both Nico Carter and Supreme shared. But until this day, they never knew it. Her name was Vandresse Lawson and although she loved them both, she was only in love with herself and it cost her everything.

"Girl, that color is poppin'. I think I need to

get that too," Tanica said, eyeing her friend's nail polish as the Chinese lady was polishing them.

"You bet not! We ain't gon' be walking around here wit' the same color polish on," Vandresse huffed.

"Won't nobody be paying attention to that shit," Tanica said, sucking her teeth.

"Stop it!" Vandresse frowned up her face as if. "You know everybody around here pay attention to what I do. All these chicks dying to be just like me," she boasted, admiring how the plum polish made her honey-colored skin pop.

Tanica glanced over at her best friend and rolled her eyes. She loved Vandresse like a sister, but at the same time Tanica felt she was so full of shit. But there was no denying, in the streets of Harlem: Vandresse was the queen of this shit. She was always the real pretty girl in the neighborhood, but once she started fuckin' with that nigga Courtney, it was on. Nobody could tell her nothing, including her childhood friend Tanica.

"I'll take that pink color," Tanica told the lady doing her nails. She had no desire to beef with Vandresse over something as simple as polish.

"So are we going to the club tonight or what?" she asked ready to talk about having some fun.

"I can't." Vandresse sighed.

"Why not? We've been talking about hitting this club since we first heard they was reopening it weeks ago."

"I know, but I told Courtney we would hang out tonight."

"Ya always hang out. Can't you spend a little time with your best friend?"

"Maybe tomorrow. I mean look at this tennis bracelet he got me." Vandresse held up her arm and slowly twirled her wrist like she was waving in a beauty pageant. "These diamonds are stunning. If I have to spend some quality time wit' my man, give him some head, sex him real good so the gifts keep coming, you gotta understand that," Vandresse explained with no filter as if the nail salon wasn't full of people, but of course she didn't give a fuck.

"I get it. I just miss hanging out with you. Brittany is cool, but she's not as fun as you," Tanica hated to admit.

"Of course she isn't, but it's not her fault. I'm the turn up queen." Vandresse laughed.

"Yeah you are." Tanica joined in on the laugh.

"But on the real. I miss hanging out with you too even though we're roommates and attend hair school together. But we haven't just hung out and had some fun like we used to. I wish Courtney had a cute friend I could hook you up with."

"Me too. Because that one you hooked me up with last time was not the answer."

"I know, but I was hoping his money would help you excuse his face," Vandresse said shrugging.

"How you luck out and get a dude who's cute and got money," Tanica stated shaking her head. "I can't believe out of all the friends Courtney got ain't none of them good looking."

"That's not true. One of his friends is a real cutie, but he just a low level worker. But he can afford to take you out to eat and buy you some sneakers... stuff like that. At least we would be able to do some double dating. If you want me to hook you up just say the word."

"Let me think about it. I don't know if I wanna sit around watching yo' man shower you wit' diamonds, all while homeboy taking me to

Footlocker, so I can pick out a new pair of Nikes."

"You so crazy." Vandresse giggled before both girls burst out laughing while continuing to chat and make jokes while finishing up at the nail salon.

"I figured you would wanna chill tonight," Vandresse said looking in the passenger side mirror as she put on some more lip gloss. "I did say I was gonna treat you extra special tonight for icing out my wrist so lovely." She smiled, using the tip of her freshly manicured nail to tap the diamonds on her tennis bracelet.

"I didn't forget. I'ma hold you to that." Courtney winked, squeezing Vandresse's bare upper thigh. "But umm, I told my man Anton I would stop by for a second. He poppin' some bottles for his birthday. Nothing major. He keepin' low key. But we do a lot of business together and I promised I come through."

"I feel you." Vandresse smiled not really caring either way. She was already plotting on how she was going to suck his dick so good tonight so she could get a diamond ring to go with her bracelet.

"But when we leave here, it's back to the crib so you can take care of Daddy." Courtney nodded.

"You know I got you, baby." Vandresse licked her lips thinking how lucky she was to have a sexy nigga who could fuck and was getting money out in these streets.

When they walked into the Uptown lounge it was jammed pack. "I thought you said this was low key," Vandresse commented.

"A lot of niggas fuck wit' Anton so they all probably coming through to show love," Courtney replied as he headed straight to the back like he knew exactly where he was going. Vandresse was right by his side, happy that she decided to wear a sexy dress tonight since there was a gang of chicks in the spot. When it came to stuntin' on other bitches, Vandresse was super competitive. She always wanted to be number one or at the very least top three.

"My nigga, C!" A guy who Vandresse assumed was the birthday boy stood up showing Courtney love.

"Happy birthday, man!" Courtney grinned. "I see everybody came out to show love to my homie."

"Yeah, I wasn't expecting all these people, but hey it's my birthday! You and your lady sit down and have some champagne," Anton said, playing the perfect host.

Courtney took Vandresse's hand so they could sit down. "Baby, I'll be right back. I need to go to the restroom. Have a glass of bubbly waiting for me when I get back," she said kissing him on the cheek.

"Excuse me, where's the restroom?" Vandresse asked one of the cocktail waitresses. The lady pointed up the stairs so Vandresse headed in that direction.

When she got to the bathroom, Vandresse was relieved nobody was in there. She wanted to check to make sure one of her tracks hadn't came loose. Vandresse always kept a needle and some thread in her purse just in case. She examined her weave and to her relief it wasn't a loose track brushing against her ear, it was her leave out. Vandresse glanced at her reflection one last time and after feeling confident she had her shit together, she exited out right as a handful of chicks were coming in.

Right in the entry way of the bathroom there was a huge spotlight. When Vandresse came in, the upstairs was damn near empty, but when she came out, there were a ton of people and all eyes seemed to be fixated on her. *Thank goodness I made sure I was straight before I walked out,* Vandresse thought to herself. She was heading back down stairs when she felt a firm grasp on her arm.

"Why the fu..." before Vandresse had a chance to curse the man out, she locked eyes with a nigga so fine she changed her mind.

"I apologize for grabbing on you, but I couldn't let you get away. You are beautiful. What's your name?"

"Vandresse," she uttered. The man's intense stare had her feeling self-conscious for some reason. Like his eyes were piercing through her soul.

"My name is Nico. Nico Carter. Come sit

down with me so we can have a drink." He spoke with so much confidence that Vandresse found herself following behind the stranger like her man wasn't downstairs waiting for her.

"I'm sorry. I can't go with you," she finally said, snapping out of her trance.

"No need to apologize. Did I do or say something to offend you?" Nico questioned.

"Not at all. I'm actually here with my man. He's downstairs waiting for me."

"Oh, really," Nico said unmoved. "That might be a problem for you tonight, but it doesn't have to be tomorrow."

Vandresse gave Nico a quizzical look. "I'm not following you."

"You're not wearing a wedding ring so you not married. Are you willing to miss out on what might be the best thing that ever happened to you?"

"Wow, you're a little full of yourself."

"Only because I have every reason to be. Give me your phone number. I'm more of an action person than a talker."

Vandresse wanted to say no because she had a good thing going with Courtney, but she also knew it wasn't a sure thing. Like Nico said, he wasn't her husband and they were both young. Vandresse wasn't stupid. She was well aware Courtney was still out there doing him. Vandresse knew she was his main bitch, but not his only chick.

"Here," she said, writing her number on a napkin then handing it to Nico.

"You're smart and beautiful. I think we'll get along just fine."

"We shall see. But I gotta go."

"Cool, I'll call you tomorrow." Nico stood at the top of the stairs looking over the banister and watched Vandresse walk over to a small group of people. A young dude stood up and took her hand and he figured that must be her man. Nico knew he needed to leave that alone, but the same way he got an adrenaline rush from dealing drugs, chasing a beautiful woman that was technically unavailable gave Nico that same high.

A KING PRODUCTION

Rich
or
Famous

Rich Because You Can Buy Fame

A NOVEL

JOY DEJA KING

Lorenzo

Welcome To My World

Before I die, if you don't remember anything else I ever taught you, know this. A man will be judged, not on what he has but how much of it. So you find a way to make money and when you think you've made enough, make some more, because you'll need it to survive in this cruel world. Money will be the only thing to save you. As I sat across from Darnell those words my father said to me on his deathbed played in my head.

"Yo, Lorenzo, are you listening to me, did you hear anything I said?"

"I heard everything you said. The problem for you is I don't give a fuck." I responded, giving a casual shoulder shrug as I rested my thumb under my chin with my index finger above my mouth.

"What you mean, you don't give a fuck? We been doing business for over three years now and that's the best you got for me?"

"Here's the thing, Darnell, I got informants all over these streets. As a matter of fact that broad you've had in your back pocket for the last few weeks is one of them."

"I don't understand what you saying," Darnell said swallowing hard. He tried to keep the tone of his voice calm, but his body composure was speaking something different.

"Alexus, has earned every dollar I've paid her to fuck wit' yo' blood suckin' ass. You a fake fuck wit' no fangs. You wanna play wit' my 100 g's like you at the casino. That's a real dummy move, Darnell." I could see the sweat beads gathering, resting in the creases of Darnell's forehead.

"Lorenzo, man, I don't know what that bitch told you but none of it is true! I swear 'bout four niggas ran up in my crib last night and took all my shit. Now that I think about it, that trifling ho Alexus probably had me set up! She fucked us both over!"

I shook my head for a few seconds not believing this muthafucker was saying that shit with a straight face. "I thought you said it was two niggas that ran up in your crib now that shit done doubled. Next thing you gon' spit is that all of Marcy projects was in on the stickup."

"Man, I can get your money. I can have it to you first thing tomorrow. I swear!"

"The thing is I need my money right now." I casually stood up from my seat and walked towards Darnell who now looked like he had been dipped in water. Watching him fall apart in front of my eyes made up for the fact that I would never get back a dime of the money he owed me.

"Zo, you so paid, this shit ain't gon' even faze you. All I'm asking for is less than twenty-four hours. You can at least give me that," Darnell pleaded.

"See, that's your first mistake, counting my pockets. My money is *my* money, so yes this shit do faze me."

"I didn't mean it like that. I wasn't tryna disrespect you. By this time tomorrow you will have your money and we can put this shit behind us." Darnell's eyes darted around in every direction instead of looking directly at me. A good liar, he was not.

"Since you were robbed of the money you owe me and the rest of my drugs, how you gon' get me my dough? I mean the way you tell it, they didn't leave you wit' nothin' but yo' dirty draws."

"I'll work it out. Don't even stress yourself, I got you, man."

"What you saying is that the nigga you so called aligned yourself with, by using my money and my product, is going to hand it back over to you?"

"Zo, what you talking 'bout? I ain't aligned myself wit' nobody. That slaw ass bitch Alexus feeding you lies."

"No, that's you feeding me lies. Why don't you admit you no longer wanted to work for me? You felt you was big shit and could be your own boss. So you used my money and product to buy your way in with this other nigga to step in my territory. But you ain't no boss you a poser. And your need to perpetrate a fraud is going to cost you your life."

"Lorenzo, don't do this man! This is all a big misunderstanding. I swear on my daughter I will have your money tomorrow. Fuck, if you let me leave right now I'll have that shit to you tonight!" I listened to Darnell stutter his words.

My men, who had been patiently waiting in each corner of the warehouse, dressed in all black, loaded with nothing but artillery, stepped out of the darkness ready to obliterate the enemy I had once considered my best worker. Darnell's eyes widened as he witnessed the men who had saved and protected him on numerous occasions, as he dealt with the vultures he encountered in the street life, now ready to end his.

"Don't do this, Zo! Pleeease," Darnell was now on his knees begging.

"Damn, nigga, you already a thief and a backstabber. Don't add, going out crying like a bitch to that too. Man the fuck up. At least take this bullet like a soldier."

"I'm sorry, Zo. Please don't do this. I gotta daughter that need me. Pleeease man, I'll do anything. Just don't kill me." The tears were pouring down Darnell's face and instead of softening me up it just made me even more pissed at his punk ass.

"Save your fuckin' tears. You shoulda thought about your daughter before you stole from me. You're the worse sort of thief. I invite you into my home, I make you a part of my family and you steal from me, you plot against me. Your daughter doesn't need you. You have nothing to teach her."

My men each pulled out their gat ready to attack and I put my hand up motioning them to stop. For the first time since Darnell arrived, a calm gaze spread across his face.

"I knew you didn't have the heart to let them kill me, Zo. We've been through so much together. I mean you Tania's God Father. We bigger than this and we will get through it," Darnell said, halfway smiling as he began getting off his knees and standing up.

"You're right, I don't have the heart to let them kill you, I'ma do that shit myself." Darnell didn't even have a chance to let what I said resonate with him because I just sprayed that muthafucker like the piece of shit he was. "Clean this shit up," I said, stepping over Darnell's bullet ridden body as I made my exit.

K. ELLIOTT'S LATEST INSTALLMENT OF

KINGPIN
Wifeys

IS ACTION PACKED AND DRAMA FILLED AS ALWAYS

Now that Shantelle is dead, will Jada be next? Was she supposed to be the one killed and not her friend? And will Shamari be there to protect her in case her life is in danger? Ava is determined not to let that happen, but is her love for her man strong enough to keep him?

Stunna has a debt to pay and until that happens, Mikhail is holding Micky as ransom. Will he pay what is owed in time to save his sister, or has he finally reached the point of no return?

TeTe is faced with a choice: taking the life of someone else, or losing her own livelihood. She is determined not to do either one, but Agent Daniels is just as determined to have it his way or now way. Who will finally come out on top?

Starr has finally gotten the man she's wanted. But did she make the right decision, and will it cost her the friendship she has built?

P.O. Box 912
Collierville, TN 38027

www.joydejaking.com
www.twitter.com/joydejaking

A King Production

ORDER FORM

Name:

Address:

City/State:

Zip:

QUANTITY	TITLES	PRICE	TOTAL
	Bitch	$15.00	
	Bitch Reloaded	$15.00	
	The Bitch Is Back	$15.00	
	Queen Bitch	$15.00	
	Last Bitch Standing	$15.00	
	Superstar	$15.00	
	Ride Wit' Me	$12.00	
	Ride Wit' Me Part 2	$15.00	
	Stackin' Paper	$15.00	
	Trife Life To Lavish	$15.00	
	Trife Life To Lavish II	$15.00	
	Stackin' Paper II	$15.00	
	Rich or Famous	$15.00	
	Rich or Famous Part 2	$15.00	
	Rich or Famous Part 3	$15.00	
	Bitch A New Beginning	$15.00	
	Mafia Princess Part 1	$15.00	
	Mafia Princess Part 2	$15.00	
	Mafia Princess Part 3	$15.00	
	Mafia Princess Part 4	$15.00	
	Mafia Princess Part 5	$15.00	
	Boss Bitch	$15.00	
	Baller Bitches Vol. 1	$15.00	
	Baller Bitches Vol. 2	$15.00	
	Baller Bitches Vol. 3	$15.00	
	Bad Bitch	$15.00	
	Still The Baddest Bitch	$15.00	
	Power	$15.00	
	Power Part 2	$15.00	
	Drake	$15.00	
	Drake Part 2	$15.00	
	Female Hustler	$15.00	
	Female Hustler Part 2	$15.00	
	Female Hustler Part 3	$15.00	
	Princess Fever "Birthday Bash"	$9.99	
	Nico Carter The Men Of The Bitch Series	$15.00	
	Bitch The Beginning Of The End	$15.00	
	Supreme...Men Of The Bitch Series	$15.00	
	Bitch The Final Chapter	$15.00	
	Stackin' Paper III	$15.00	
	Men Of The Bitch Series And The Women Who Love Them	$15.00	
	Coke Like The 80s	$15.00	

Shipping/Handling (Via Priority Mail) $6.50 1-2 Books, $8.95 3-4 Books add $1.95 for ea. Additional book.

Total: $_____FORMS OF ACCEPTED PAYMENTS: Certified or government issued checks and money Orders, all ma~
in orders take 5-7 Business days to be delivered